La Belle Roumaine

Dumitru Tsepeneag

LA BELLE ROUMAINE

Translated from the Romanian by Alistair Ian Blyth

DALKEY ARCHIVE PRESS

Originally published in Romanian by Editura Paralela 45 as *La belle Roumaine* in 2004.

First Dalkey Archive edition, 2017.

Library of Congress Cataloging-in-Publication Data
Names: Tsepeneag, Dumitru, 1937- author. | Blyth, Alistair Ian, translator.
Title: La belle roumaine / by Dumitru Tsepeneag ; translated from the Romanian by Alistair Ian Blyth.
Other titles: Belle roumaine. English
Description: First Dalkey Archive edition. | Victoria, TX : Dalkey Archive Press, 2017.
Identifiers: LCCN 2017006157 | ISBN 9781943150304 (pbk. : alk. paper)
Subjects: LCSH: Women--Europe--Fiction. | False personation--Europe--Fiction. | Jews--Identity--Fiction.
Classification: LCC PC840.3.E67 B4513 2017 | DDC 859/.334--dc23
LC record available at https://lccn.loc.gov/2017006157

Partially funded by the Translation Publication Support Program of the Romanian Cultural Institute.

www.dalkeyarchive.com
Victoria, TX / McLean, IL / Dublin

Dalkey Archive Press publications are, in part, made possible through the support of the University of Houston-Victoria and its programs in creative writing, publishing, and translation.

Printed on permanent/durable acid-free paper

Life must not be a novel that is given to us,
but a novel that is made by us.
Novalis, *Fragments*

SHE ALWAYS SAT DOWN at the same table. Hard to say how she found it vacant every time. Especially in the beginning or, to be more exact, on the first three days: nobody else occupied the table before she arrived. It was, let us say, mere chance. On the following days, however, it was no longer down to chance, but to Jean-Jacques, the proprietor, who made sure the table remained vacant, so convinced was he that the beautiful blond would continue to come. Conviction, or rather desire: the two came together in his mind and led him to behave in such a way that he ran the risk of looking odd in the eyes of his regular customers. But since he also performed the job of barman, he could hardly have been expected not to keep a watch over the more or less aleatory movements of his customers; he could hardly have been expected, on occasion, not to intervene:

—You can't sit here, he'd say. This table is reserved.

The customer seemed a little taken aback. He was holding a rolled-up newspaper: no, not *Le Monde*, but *Paris-Turf*, on which you could see just the picture of a horse's head, with blinkers, those leather flaps required by more timorous racehorses; they don't like running in a pack, and the blinkers force them to look ahead, not to the side. Jean-Jacques nodded to show that he was well aware of the ruse. That way, the horse thinks he's the only one on the grass of the racetrack; mettlesome and left to his own devices, he's unstressed by the thought of any competition. The customer's explanations were rather persuasive. But even so, as the barman later thought, during the race the horse on the track couldn't help but feel the humanoid clinging like the devil to his back, as well as swatting him at intervals with a flexible rod sheathed in leather. The horse couldn't help but feel that alien will, which manifested itself in the form of blows, each more painful than the last . . .

Jean-Jacques was a well-built man, who might be said to have looked older than he really was. In other words, his appearance couldn't help but instill a certain amount of deference on the part of his customers. And so the other man, the customer with the *Paris-Turf*, looked at him closely, wishing to ascertain whether he was pulling his leg. But the other man's expression was completely serious; he didn't look like he was in the mood for jokes.

—Reserved? said the racetrack punter in surprise.

—Yes, yes, this table is reserved. Don't insist.

—Well, then put a reserved sign there, a label, something, so that we'll know what's what, mumbled the customer, since he too would have liked to sit at that particular table every now and then and read his newspaper.

To be sure, the table was perfectly positioned: neither too close to the glass front of the small bistro that Jean-Jacques grandly called a café nor too far, but rather mid-stage, in the shade of the coatrack where the beautiful stranger hung her fur coat, an item still necessary in that colder-than-usual February weather. They say that women are crazy for mink, but some deem silver fox to be even more chic. It was likely that that fur coat, made from the tails of silver foxes, had also to a certain extent augmented the barman's admiration of the woman, who, in his opinion, looked like one of those actresses from pre-war films. Now they were real women! Beautiful, elegant, endowed with all the necessities . . .

She was beautiful, and then some! The perfectly regular features of her face came together to form a likeable and intelligent physiognomy, even if occasionally her turquoise eyes stared into empty space and she slightly clenched her lips. You would have thought that she was unhappy or that she was brooding on thoughts not exactly rosy. Who knows what unbearable memories afflicted her, who knows what cruel past held her captive even now . . . This was why she didn't look as young as she was beautiful. But fortunately for her and all the café's other customers, that rictus appeared quite seldom and vanished very quickly.

Her table was therefore perfectly visible from the bar, where Jean-Jacques was keeping himself busy with this and that. But he didn't venture to look at her directly, to fasten her with his gaze for a few long moments, as he very easily would have been able to do from the strategic position he occupied. He contented himself with casting quick sidelong glances. You might say that he was eating her up with his eyes, but in brief bursts. He was pecking at her . . .

She never stayed for more than half an hour. She usually ordered a cup of coffee, with just a drop of milk, and sometimes, but seldom, a croissant. She had a grave voice, with an accent that Jean-Jacques had difficulty placing.

No, it wasn't an Italian accent, with which Jean-Jacques was familiar. He'd been to Italy many times when he was a young man and had subsequently had an amorous liaison with a woman from Florence, who had vanished without trace in the end. They'd met in Paris and lived together for only a few weeks. Even so, he'd eventually gotten it into his head to marry her. To this end, Silvia went back to Florence and Jean-Jacques was to have gone there to meet her parents. When he got off the train in Florence, Silvia wasn't waiting for him on the platform as she'd promised. And Jean-Jacques didn't know her address. He knew only that her name was Silvia Burlesconi. He looked it up in a telephone directory: no one by the name of Burlesconi. "It's a rare name," Silvia had explained . . . "Not only are there few of them, but they don't even have a telephone!" thought Jean-Jacques in vexation. He left the railway station and walked around the surrounding streets for a short while. He ate a pizza. Excellent! He ordered an espresso. He couldn't be bothered to act the tourist. A Japanese woman gave him a winsome look. She came up to him, nonchalantly swinging her camera. Maybe she took him for a local and wanted to ask directions . . . Jean-Jacques turned on his heel and headed for the station to find out when the first train back to Paris would be leaving.

The next day he returned to his native city with his tail between his legs. For a week he didn't leave the house. At the time he was still living with his mother. She had to look after the bistro more or less single-handedly. The poor woman was in despair when she saw Jean-Jacques lying motionless all day long, staring up at the ceiling. What was he waiting for? Silvia sent no word. She'd completely vanished. Probably something had happened to her, some dreadful misfortune. She'd lost her life in a car accident. The driver had lost control and crashed into a petrol tanker. He was a lover of hers, insanely jealous of Jean-Jacques. She'd just informed him of her intention to marry the Frenchman and settle in Paris.

Or else she'd been kidnapped by the Mafia and packed off to Africa, where she now eked out her days in a Maghreb brothel. Or else she'd been murdered . . . By her own father, a fanatical far-right militant, who couldn't endure the thought of his own daughter marrying a Frenchman, and a member of the Communist Party to boot. Who knows . . . During those days, Jean-Jacques came up with the most outlandish plots for novels. It was an occupation that exhausted him. It would seem that because of this, for a long time afterward, he was unable to read any more novels. Another effect of this debauch of the imagination was ultimately beneficial: in his mind, riddled with doubts and exhausted by so great a narrative exertion, Silvia gradually shed any consistent reality; all that remained of her was a shadow, and a formless one at that: a gray blotch in the darkness and finally nothing at all . . . Perhaps she'd never really existed, in fact, as Jean-Jacques said to himself one night, alone in his cold, damp bed.

And so, the beautiful stranger didn't speak with the accent so characteristic of Italians, as he'd at first been tempted to believe. To tell the truth, there was nothing Italian-looking about her at all. She rather looked Slavic . . . And not only because she was a blond and had blue eyes. German women are blonds, too, and they have blue eyes as well. So do Swedish and Danish women. Nordic women in general. And let's not forget English women. Then again, he couldn't be sure that her golden hair was in fact dyed or at least bleached. Therefore, it wasn't just a question of her hair or her eyes, but something else besides, something hard to explain.

Jean-Jacques had an assistant. His name was Ed, a young man, blondish, rather chubby, around nineteen or twenty years old, perhaps older, who served tables at peak hours, especially at lunchtime. Otherwise, Jean-Jacques managed on his own. He served both at the tables and behind the counter. There weren't many tables: nine or ten. But even so, there were times when he felt overwhelmed. He'd run back and forth, mumbling about what he'd do to that Ed, who had either not turned up, even though it was almost lunchtime, or wasn't even due at work, although it was still at him that Jean-Jacques directed his ire. He could barely cope. What annoyed him the most was that he no longer found the time to chat with the customers he was serving at the tables. In that respect, the ones who sat at the bar were privileged, in particular Yegor, who almost never opted for a table. He leaned his elbows on the countertop and didn't even look at the other customers inside the café. Probably they didn't interest him. And why would they? He chatted to the barman about everything under the sun. It was enough for him. But Jean-Jacques had to keep his eyes peeled, he had to be on the lookout for every movement, for the gestures specific to the customers, who got annoyed if they weren't paid sufficient attention. And so, as he talked to Yegor, he kept an eye on the other customers, kept the front door under surveillance. Distributive attention, a perspicacious eye, a sense of rhythm: a true orchestra conductor!

—Here at last! shouted Jean-Jacques when Ed finally made his appearance. I've been waiting . . .

—Her voice is like Elvire Popesco's, said Jean-Jacques, pointlessly rinsing an already-washed glass.

—Like whose?

—Like Elvire Popesco's! The actress . . .

—Must be Russian . . .

And as he smiled, Yegor's moustache would have given a twitch, had he had one. What he did have, however, was a rapidly spreading bald patch. Every morning he found dislodged hairs on his pillow.

—What do you mean, Russian! Isn't Elvire Popesco Romanian?

—I was joking . . . I heard she tried to put on a Russian accent. On stage . . .

—That's right.

—But why?

—I don't know.

—I'll tell you why. Because she was cast as women from the East, from where it's cold, from Russia, in other words . . .

—It's cold in Romania, too, in winter . . .

—You can hardly compare Romanian with Russian cold. Besides, Romania is, how can I put it? It's no great shakes. People have only heard of it because of its dictator, the notorious Ceaușescu. His wife Elena was more famous than the actress.

—That may be . . . But what about in the past? In the days of Elvire Popesco? What I mean is when the actress was at the height of her glory . . . before the war, during the war and immediately after . . . Back then, Ceaușescu was a nobody!

—I've no idea. She was before my time.

—Before your time?

—I've never seen her on stage.

—She doesn't act anymore, true. But if you want to see her, you should do your utmost to attend her salon on avenue Foch . . . She's very old, but she hasn't given up, she still receives every Thursday.

—Have you been?

—No, I haven't. But I heard about it from somebody, a journalist. You, on the other hand, given that you belong to such an important nation . . .

—There's no point in your making fun of me. Anyway, admit it, compared with Russia, Romania barely exists. Not to mention that it's a country of gypsies and fraudsters.

—Gypsies, agreed! But fraudsters . . . What fraudsters?

—Take the famous Manolescu; Thomas Mann wrote about him.

Jean-Jacques wasn't sure who Thomas Mann was, being less educated than his friend, but that didn't stop him giving a common-sense answer:

—Let's be honest: this Manolescu of yours doesn't exist . . .

—How so?

—Well, if I understand rightly, he's a character in a novel.

—What does it matter! Behind it, behind every novel, there's always something real. It didn't just fall from the clear blue sky, the novelist didn't just dream it . . . Probably he took the character from some news item or somebody told him about him. He needed a fraudster and he dubbed him Manolesco. Did he come up with the name or was the real fraudster really called that? I have no idea. Dostoevsky used the same method with his characters. Understand? He took them from news items . . .

—Didn't he change the names?

—Yes, he did, I think, but how am I supposed to know . . . What does it matter? Maybe the fraudster from the news item wasn't called Manolesco, but something else, I don't know, Ionesco or Popesco, for example.

In the end, Jean-Jacques let himself be persuaded. Or at least he pretended to be persuaded, so that Yegor would shut up about it. Yegor was Russian by birth and felt an infectious disdain for the land of Elvire Popesco. Maybe even for her too! Otherwise, why would he criticize her Russian accent? And besides, that accent of hers was a bit of a caricature. But even so, what Yegor said didn't really stand up, if you thought about it a little more, since apparently Elvire Popesco spoke in the same accent even when she wasn't on stage. She used the same accent when she was out and about town. In her salon. In bed! Ha, ha, ha! When she made love, she did so with a Russian accent. What went on in that little head of hers? Probably she felt humiliated that her country meant next to nothing to the French, who, on the other hand, at least since the defeat at Berezina, were fearful of vast Russia and had even come to worship it. You French like a Russian accent? All right then! A Russian accent you shall have, with bells on too . . . Some might claim that her accent was not authentic. So what! Who could check on its authenticity anyway? Only the Russians. But Russians and Frenchmen of Russian origin were rather delighted that an actress of Elvire Popesco's stature spoke French with a so-called Russian accent. And so they kept their mouths shut, they didn't criticize her accent, they didn't betray her, they even spread a rumor that she was in fact Moldavian, and that the letters she wrote to her parents back home were in Cyrillic script. In other words, she belonged to the large family of nations who lived under Russian tutelage. Perhaps they didn't put it in quite such terms, but anyway . . . People say all kinds of things. Did such idle chatter reach the ears of the actress? Probably. What of it! In any event, it's hard to know how people react or what motivates them, even when they're public figures. It's highly likely that Elvire Popesco would have wished to shed her Romanian accent, and because she couldn't acquire, as if by miracle, a bona fide French accent, she opted for that of the speakers of a language better known than her mother tongue, a language spoken by a far more numerous nation, one that inspires respect, if not fear (ultimately they're the same thing!), a nation that was trying to construct a fairer society, in which all men would be equal. True, in the end they didn't quite succeed, but that was because the whole world was against them. The Germans, first of all, and then the Americans . . . The whole world put spokes in their wheels! The Germans attacked them; the Americans first helped them and then constantly threatened them. There was no end of accusations, from every side: Stalin, the Gulag, everything under the sun. Some of them true. What of it! What else could they have done? How about their accusers try constructing a new society with old-style people! Where were they supposed to get hold of new-style people? Whether they liked it or not, the children were raised by old-style people. And ultimately, even the leaders, the ones who, out of conformism more than anything else, were ensconced at the top of the Party and government, even they were old-style people. That's the truth of it! Old-style people who didn't believe in what they were doing. They were self-serving; they did what they did to make things cozy for themselves or to slake their thirst for power.

He shared none of these thoughts with Yegor, who held political opinions that were completely different. Yegor grew heated when he gave voice to his opinions, particularly when he got onto the subject of China. Whenever he talked about China or the United States, with that President Reagan of theirs, who had sunk the Soviets. And then there was their current president . . . But the deed was done, Bush was merely reaping the benefits. Yegor went on and on . . . In the end, he'd even make himself out to be disgusted by politics.

—With you, everything comes down to politics, Yegor would say, getting annoyed, and he'd knock back his (overly small) glass of vodka.

—Well, doesn't it?

—I for one am sick of politics. After all I lived through in Russia . . .

—You mean to say that you lot had a political life over there? Don't make me laugh!

He contradicts himself, this Jean-Jacques of ours! But it wasn't easy for him either. Particularly given that so many things had happened in world politics in the last few years that he couldn't make head or tail of it all, he couldn't put it in any logical order, or at least not in any order that fit his ideas and beliefs, which themselves were perhaps also starting to shift.

To tell the truth, there were a number of other topics that Jean-Jacques not only avoided broaching, but quite simply refused to continue discussing if by any chance he got onto one of them. One such topic was Italy. Yegor would have liked to talk about Italy, a country he'd been to a few times and of which he had very pleasant memories. But he quickly realized that the same couldn't be said of Jean-Jacques. One day, not long after they first met, looking at the bottles on the shelf, Yegor said with a smile, just on the off chance:

—I can't understand why you don't have a bottle of grappa in your collection. It's an excellent drink, you know . . .

Jean-Jacques turned his back and pretended not to hear. Yegor repeated the question and Jean-Jacques still made no reply.

—I see you've got something against Italy, Yegor mused aloud, and this time Jean-Jacques curtly replied:

—It's not a country I'm interested in!

Yegor hadn't been living in the neighborhood very long. At first, he'd frequented another bistro, next to the Métro station, which was kept by a personable woman, but who would start to frown when she came to pour him his third glass of vodka. Her brow furrowed, her eyebrows lowered, and her hand shook as if she were ill with Parkinson's disease as she decanted the precious liquid. When the customer asked for a fifth glass, his request fell on deaf ears and he'd be left with outstretched hand, like a beggar. His repeated requests became pleas and then lamentations. In vain! She'd go into the kitchen, come back, look in a completely different direction. Yegor naturally lost patience. Worse still, toward the end of the spectacle he'd feel exhausted, irritated . . . Even if he finally obtained his umpteenth glass of vodka, he still didn't escape the lady's muttered litany of disapproval. Her exhortations to moderation were insufferable to him, all the more so given that they were accompanied and illustrated by the tragic tale of her son, who had died of liver cancer not long before.

—Did he drink vodka?

—No, he drank only wine . . .

—Well then!

The poor mother choked with indignation. The offhand, mocking tone of the drinker in front of her quite simply made her blow her top.

—We don't serve people in a state of inebriation, she said, furiously, and still grasping her dishcloth, she swept her arm over the zinc countertop, sending two glasses flying. The glasses hurtled into a shelf full of liquor bottles and smashed with such a loud noise that all the customers in the bistro turned to look. Some of them approached, curious to see what had happened. Some burst into laughter, while others took Madame Renard's side, particularly given that they believed the vodka drinker himself had broken the glasses because he was so drunk. Yegor defended himself as best he could:

—My dear madam, I'm not drunk. I'm perfectly sober. And what is more, I can assure you I didn't come by car. I don't even have one. Neither a car nor a motorbike. I don't know how to drive. Besides, your glasses are so small that you can't even taste the drink. You're a little strange, that's for sure! How do you expect me to get drunk with such small glasses . . .

—If you don't like my glasses, then go on, sling your hook! Go somewhere else! yelled the poor woman.

The next day, the waster was back again. As straight as a ramrod. Reporting for duty.

—Where are you from? the lady would sometimes ask, sympathetically.

—From around the corner.

—I meant, what country are you from . . .

Yegor didn't like that type of question. Granted, he knew that no matter what, his accent would give him away, but even though he'd obtained French citizenship five years previously and had been in France for around ten years, people still asked him what country he was from. Morbid curiosity? Not a bit of it! Just regular curiosity . . . Some people guessed it for themselves, since they were familiar with the Russian accent, or rather caricatures thereof. They at least had a notion of what accent it might be. But they went ahead and asked anyway, just to confirm it. People need to be reassured of their opinions. Perhaps because they're so unsure of themselves . . . And then, interest in people's origins is a throwback to childhood, when we're utterly obsessed with it. Which explains children's anguish when they're told, obviously in jest, that they were stolen and sold by the gypsies. Let us pass over the racism inherent in that, since there's not much we can do about it . . . What's more interesting is to examine the idea that to lose one's origins is, in people's minds, tantamount to exile from paradise. Not flight from paradise! The word is too weak . . . Even exile is saying too little. It's a fall, a vertiginous fall! That's the most fitting phrase. In moral terms: decadence. As far as Yegor was concerned, he was an exile, a genuine fallen angel, the people around him sensed it very well, they were fearful of him and at the same time pitied him.

—I'm a French citizen! cried Yegor. After which he'd say, with deliberate irony: Would you like to see my ID card?

No, nobody wished to see it. The French are discreet and

polite. At least that's how they like to depict themselves. Anyway, they're not born detectives. They're more like concierges, yes, increasingly so . . .

—Are you a Yugoslav by chance? the tavern keeper went on.

That's how Yegor referred to her, by way of revenge, but for a long time the term remained pallid in his mind, it didn't acquire any acoustic consistency until much later, when he changed tavern and befriended Jean-Jacques, to whom he recounted his adventures around Paris. Jean-Jacques had a weakness for people from the East, and for Russians in particular.

—Why'd you avoid telling her the truth? asked Jean-Jacques, even later still, when Yegor brought up Madame Renard once again.

The Russian didn't answer straightaway. He ran his fingers through his wavy hair. No, he wasn't blond; his hair was rather chestnut brown, with a single gold-colored lock. A sparser and sparser chestnut brown . . .

—I don't know. I find it annoying to be questioned like that. I'm not in a police cell.

—Fine, fine, we're not in a police cell, but how do you expect to have a conversation if we can't ask questions?

—You're right . . .

—I ask you questions, too. True, you don't always answer.

—You're my friend. Even if I don't answer, I don't get annoyed.

—That's the limit: it's still you who gets annoyed!

—Who else?

—Hang on! Look, she's coming . . .

—Who?

—The blond I was telling you about . . . Shush! Shut up a minute!

Without hesitation the woman headed to her table, vacant thanks to Jean-Jacques, who had spent the whole morning making sure nobody occupied it. Yegor cast her a long glance, at the same time sniffing his empty vodka glass. He thrust his nose inside the glass, which, although small, was sufficiently capacious to contain the Russian olfactory organ. Having plonked her sack-sized handbag on a chair, the blond took off her fur coat and, standing on tiptoes, hung it up. She wouldn't have needed to stand on tiptoes had she been content to hang it on one of the lower pegs. But probably she was stretching on purpose, to show off the perfect shape of her body to the males in the café, her steatopygous bottom, her contours, highlighted by her dungarees, made from a material that was a mix of artificial fibers, but also some silk. The dungarees clung tightly to her body, which fit as if she'd been poured into them.

—A tidy piece of tackle, no denying it! Pour me another drink.

Jean-Jacques took his glass without a word. You could see he was tense from a mile off. He kept his eyes lowered, naturally, so as not to miss the glass and spill the drink. Yegor started teasing him.

—Back home in Russia there are loads of blonds like her . . .

—Screw you! muttered Jean-Jacques.

She'd sat down at the table and was now smoking a cigarette and looking fixedly at the bar. Jean-Jacques mechanically went on wiping the countertop with a sponge. Finally, he ventured to look up at the lady customer, who took advantage of the opportunity to make her order.

—A coffee, please! And a glass of water . . .

Yegor, who had in the meantime been sitting with his back to her, turned around once more and gave her a smile that stretched from ear to ear. The woman responded with a flash of her teeth, which were markedly less white than the ones on those billboards that extol such and such a brand of toothpaste. What's more, her hair hadn't been blond from birth, but was more than certainly dyed. Yegor had a trained eye; seldom did he err. Her hair hadn't been raven black, but rather light chestnut, in any case not as flaxen as it was now. In the meantime, Jean-Jacques was drawing off coffee from the little faucet of the percolator. There was no conceivable way he could have seen the smiles the other two were exchanging behind his back. Why then was his hand trembling so badly that he spilled a few drops in the saucer on which he was trying to place the coffee cup? He took another saucer. Leaning on his elbows, Yegor mockingly watched Jean-Jacques's shaky movements. He was no longer looking at the woman, who had just taken a book out of her handbag. Yegor was focused on Jean-Jacques and followed him with his eyes as he went to the beautiful stranger's table. Absorbed in her book, the woman paid no attention to Jean-Jacques as he cautiously placed the coffee cup on the table. He'd forgotten the glass of water, and so he went back to the bar.

—What's she reading? asked Yegor.

—A book in German about Europe.

—In German?

—Yes, in German.

—Then she's German . . .

Jean-Jacques gave an irritated shrug. What did her nationality matter when she was there in the flesh and blood, beneath his very eyes! With calm and dignity, he went back to the customer's table, bringing the glass of water. She enveloped him with her blue-eyed gaze, measuring him from head to toe. She then murmured a thank-you. Jean-Jacques withdrew, moving backwards.

Meanwhile, the eyes of another customer had been drinking up the scene or rather the female character cast in the principal rôle. He was holding an unfolded copy of *Paris-Turf*, but without reading it. At the same time, he was looking at Yegor, who, behind the barman, was casting winsome smiles at the woman and, at one point, even gave her a wink, together with a hand gesture. She made no perceptible reaction. She seemed preoccupied with the trembling hands of the barman, who had brought her glass of water. In the café, silence had fallen. An unusual silence.

***

Johannes gave an indulgent laugh whenever she said something stupid, he took her hand and kissed it or gave her a paternal or rather a protective, friendly peck on the forehead: he wasn't much older than her, perhaps he wasn't older at all. It was hard to say how old that mysterious woman from the mouths of the Danube was . . . The fascination she exerted on men was also due to the uncertainty in which she was able to keep them for the longest possible time. This was why she let herself be pampered and exaggerated her naivety, her candor; she could see very well that it was something the German liked . . . Why not let him take pleasure in it? She strove to endear herself to him in every way, both at the table and in the sheets. Especially given that he wasn't demanding. He was grateful to her and, for his part, he forced himself to overlook other, less agreeable things, he pretended not to notice them, kept his nose in his philosophy books, and sometimes he even managed not to register any of the things that might have troubled him. He read avidly, making conscientious notes. From time to time he'd pause and look out of the window. The sky was blue. And he was striving to be as serene as possible . . .

That day it seemed to her that she'd seen Mihai in the Métro. In one of the passageways to be precise. Perhaps it was really he . . . But there were a lot of people and she'd lost sight of him. Anyhow, if Mihai were in Paris he'd have telephoned her. This was why she was in a very good mood when she entered the café. She traversed the space between the door and her table distributing smiles left and right. Leaning on the countertop, for the umpteenth time Yegor was telling Jean-Jacques the story of how he'd left Madame Renard.

—She wasn't a bad woman, believe me, but she was doing my head in. Understand?

Jean-Jacques was listening with only one ear. All the rest of his being was focused in the direction of the woman who had just come through the door and, with a swaying, nonchalant walk, was approaching the table kept vacant, ready for her. She didn't seem at all surprised. Did she think it was normal that she should always find the table vacant? And why did she never go to another table? Why was she not tempted to sit by the window, for example, now that the weather was getting quite warm and she had no reason to fear the cold outside?

Her gestures had become increasingly precise. True, they were the same gestures she'd made so many times before. She rid herself of her handbag and then her trench coat, which she hung up on the peg. This time, she was wearing a short, tight skirt. She no longer concealed her legs. On the contrary. And quite rightly so, since she had splendid legs: they were far from being slender, but nor were they too thick; the round, well-honed knees betokened long but generous, welcoming thighs. She sat down. She took a deep breath and looked around her, smiling. From her handbag she took a handkerchief, wiped her brow, lips, nose. Then she took out a book, a different one than last time, and on the cover Jean-Jacques thought to glimpse the famous bridge between the Louvre and the Académie. He was almost sure of it.

—If she carries on like this, she'll lose most of her customers. If she doesn't lose them, then it means the French are special, a bit masochistic, I mean . . .

Naturally, Yegor was talking about Madame Renard. But Jean-Jacques couldn't give a toss about Madame Renard. He was no longer listening to him. He went over to the beautiful blond to take her order. His hawk-like eyes hadn't been mistaken: on the cover of the book could be seen the Pont des Arts, photographed from the Louvre side. Glinting in the sun, the Académie cupola was unmistakeable. The barman's admiration increased by yet another degree. The woman was moving her lips, and

Jean-Jacques pricked up his ears. He then gave an abrupt bow, as if he'd taken a punch to the stomach. He went back next to Yegor and panting, murmured in his ear:

—She's ordered a vodka . . .

Yegor didn't react right away. He remained with his head lowered, like a boxer taking advantage of his opponent's last blow in order to gain a respite, if only for an instant, leaning his back against the ropes. He waited for Jean-Jacques to fill the glass, to place it on a saucer, and then on a small tray, with smiling and slightly affected care, and then he said:

—I'll take it to her.

—No way! It's not your job!

Yegor didn't push it. It would've been pointless anyhow. Jean-Jacques cast him a dark look and scuttled off. Yegor strove to suppress his excitement. He sat motionless, contenting himself with a long glance at Jean-Jacques, who, in a manner brimming with elegance, based, evidently, on vast experience, was now proffering the tray: his bust inclined at an angle of around forty degrees, one arm held slightly to the rear, by his hip, the other holding aloft the glass on its platter—a motionless waiter, his head bowed, but his eyes wide open, in order to gaze at the woman's legs, knees and thighs, which he divined to be substantial, but not overly muscular. What was already visible beneath the hitched-up skirt was enormously promising, particularly to the kind of man who continued to conceive of the female body in, let us say, a "classic" manner. She was reading without making the slightest movement. Her face was impassive. She seemed absorbed in her book. After a few seconds, Jean-Jacques straightened up and, with great delicacy, grasped the glass with just two fingers to place it in front of the book, whose reader was now resting it against the edge of the table in order to make room for the receptacle containing the vodka. It was full to the brim. Jean-Jacques became flustered: he'd forgotten to lift the saucer from the tray. He realized his mistake and immediately rectified it. Finally, she deigned to look at him. And to smile at him. Benevolently.

She hated flying. Yes, she was afraid of a plane crash. She wasn't the only one. What were the statistics? No, he didn't know them. Are there more car crashes than plane crashes? Yes, all too possible . . . why not? What about train crashes? Really? Come on . . .

It may well be, she said, but with a little luck you can survive a car or a train crash, whereas . . .

She didn't necessarily want to contradict him, she was replying more out of politeness than anything else, just to keep the conversation going. She smiled at the man on the seat opposite her.

—You survive, said the traveler, who was a large man, mechanically rubbing his forehead and the beginnings of a bald patch, you survive, but in what state? Paralyzed, in a wheelchair, mutilated for life, disfigured . . . You'd be better off dead!

He had some serious arguments there and no mistake! She nodded and seemed to be letting herself be more and more persuaded. In any event, she was making an effort to that effect. Nonetheless, she admitted, in her case, it wasn't only fear of an air crash. She also took the train because she liked traveling by train. In the first place, it was much more comfortable than traveling by car. Not to mention by plane. In a plane you sit there cramped, unable to move from your seat; you have no more space than a hen in some ultramodern factory farm. And besides, she liked to hear the train wheels rumbling along the rails . . . She found the sound of that rumbling pleasant. Did he?

No, he didn't. In the first place, train wheels no longer sounded like they did in the old days. It was a rumbling in name only. Nowadays all you can hear is a kind of swishing.

—Listen! . . .

There was a pause in the conversation. She looked at the birdcage: the eagle chick was fidgeting; it couldn't keep still.

—Is that a parrot?

She tittered and made no reply. She was now looking out of the window, in a slightly dreamy sort of way, although there was nothing much to see: a gloomy winter landscape, without any snow, which made it look even more sinister. She was no longer paying very much attention to what her fellow traveler was saying. After asking what kind of bird it was—in jest, obviously—he'd returned to the subject of accidents and their consequences. She liked talking to him, but by now she was sick of the same subject, which he'd been going on and on about for the last half an hour. And here he was carrying on the same conversation, still talking about accidents. Since he was saying something about children's apparent unconcern when it came to accidents, or rather the possibility thereof, she took the opportunity to change the subject to childhood, to her childhood, which had been the happiest time of her life. The German nodded his head in agreement. Was it for him, too?

—Yes, sure . . . Childhood . . .

A happiness cut short by a horrifying event, however: her twin sister had been kidnapped by a pedophile.

—A pedophile? Did he kill her or just . . .

—He raped her and then killed her.

—In the Ceaușescu period?

—No, shortly before that, in the Gheorghiu-Dej period. She was called Mariette, which comes from Maria. Her name was Maria, mine is Ana . . . Or Annette . . .

—Far too little is known about that period, said the German. But all kinds of things happened back then, each more dreadful than the next . . .

Probably the German was more interested in politics than childhood. But she wasn't discouraged and said a few more things about the event that not only shattered her childhood, but continued to scar her life, since not even now, after so many years, was she able to forget, all she could manage was not to think about it for a while, and when she did remember once more, she was filled with horror. The German nodded compassionately, but he didn't ask her any question that might extend the conversation, prompt her to say more, add further details, as she herself would probably have wished, although she didn't dare to do so, seeing very well that the man opposite her was listening only out of politeness and by no means out of curiosity. He'd have wished to talk about Gheorghiu-Dej and the Romanian Communist Party . . .

It wouldn't be long before they arrived in Paris, at the Gare de l'Est. The German was becoming more and more excited, although it wasn't the first time he'd been to Paris. "The most beautiful city in the world!" he enthused. Neither Vienna, nor London, nor Rome could compare with Paris! She put on her fur coat and glimpsed an admiring gleam in the man's eyes.

Before the train pulled into the station, he tore a page from a notebook and wrote down the telephone number at which he could be reached. And his name: Wolfgang, which he'd already told her during the course of the conversation. She was unable to reciprocate and tried to explain why. She didn't have a telephone yet . . . She didn't know where she'd be living yet. But he was in a hurry or in fact wasn't very interested.

—Yes, very well, said Wolfgang. Very well . . .

He'd stood up already and was looking out of the window of the train carriage. As he was tall, his head was almost level with the birdcage, against whose bars the eagle chick was busily grating its beak. Wolfgang opened the window to get a better view. Ana looked out of the window too. Somebody was indeed waiting for him on the platform: a tall man with a moustache, who was wearing a padded raincoat and a hat, and holding an Alsatian on a leash.

Jean-Jacques dreamed of her the whole night. Between two dreams he masturbated without managing to reach a climax.

But it helped him to procure additional details for what was now a recurring dream. It never recurred identically, however. Variations cropped up, whence the need for details.

With the tip of his toes he pushed open a door as light as a curtain. A red door. The whole dream was a gliding, forward motion. He entered a room where there was a bed that filled almost the whole space. Lolling on the bed, in a silvery-white nightdress as frothy as champagne, was the beautiful stranger herself, whom he called now Elvire, now Elena. Or perhaps both women were there, one after the other or simultaneously . . . In a flickering light the color of calvados. At the foot of the bed a black dog bared its fangs, but without making any particular effort to look more menacing. It bared its slobbering fangs and that was all . . . A little way away, on a low table, there was a birdcage with a huge parrot, a kind of toucan. It had a great big beak and garish colors: red, yellow, and blue. In just his long johns, Jean-Jacques advanced toward the bed, approached the woman. She raised herself on one elbow, a plump, slithering mermaid, and craned her head forward, her mouth wide open. It was no wonder that Jean-Jacques was completely swallowed up inside the mouth, which was as big as a barn and gave onto another room where, sprawling on a bed as spacious as the one before, could be found the other woman, Elena, fleshless, pale, as hideous as death. She awaited him motionless.

On the sill of a window that opened onto the darkness of night was a bronze-colored eagle, about to take flight . . . Jean-Jacques took a step backward. Fear had seeped to his very innards.

He awoke.

The next day, he thought about recounting his dream to Yegor. On further reflection, however, he changed his mind. It's impossible to narrate a dream. It yields nothing. When narrated, a dream is impoverished; it shrivels like a jellyfish cast up on the sand. This is why we're never satisfied when we narrate a dream. It's pointless our narrating it, since we're no longer in the dream; we're elsewhere. We get annoyed. We feel the need to invent a host of details, to add something of our own, to specify the circumstances and describe the places that fit our dream, in order thereby to make the narrative more concrete, more believable, closer to the real dream that's dissolving in our memory, losing its colors and even that so characteristic oneiric light. Sometimes we feel we've succeeded to some extent, but this is because we've introduced a certain logical concatenation, which distances us yet farther from the dream we really experienced. The result is something unusual, sometimes something very interesting, strange and beautiful, but it isn't our nocturnal dream. But enough blather. The dream can't be narrated: we have to present it, reconstruct it, write it, rewrite it, fabricate it from start to finish. The real dream, the nocturnal dream, can only be a model for oneiric narrative. It supplies only the laws, the structure, but not the matter. Which is to say, the subject . . .

He wasn't going to recount his dream to Yegor. No way!

Two or three days later, Yegor and the beautiful stranger turned up at the café together. The man pushed open the door with his shoulder and then stepped aside for the woman, who entered with her head held high and her hands stuffed in her pockets. She looked like an American actress newly arrived from Hollywood. Although the weather was warming up, she was wearing her fur coat again. Jean-Jacques stared at them as if he couldn't believe his eyes. He stood there with his mouth agape. Poor Jean-Jacques! Hard to say what was going on in his mind right then. The simplest thing for him would have been to imagine that the two had bumped into each other outside the café: Yegor had probably greeted her with a bow, overdoing the bow a little and thereby running the risk of it being interpreted as ironic, but nonetheless the woman had smiled at him, she was amused, and she entered the café in front of him, with swaying gait, wrapped up in her silver fox fur. The man then quickly closed the door behind them both.

And this indeed had been more or less the way of it . . . But with the important distinction that Yegor had seen her from a distance and deliberately slowed his steps, he'd even stopped for a few moments, pretending to throw a crumpled wad of paper in a litter bin, after which he continued to pause at intervals, under various pretexts, so that they'd both reach the door of the café at the same time. Obviously, she'd noticed the whole strategem, which was why she didn't linger to look at the window of the porcelain shop, as she'd been tempted to do, nor did she go inside the bookshop where she usually bought her books. She strode toward the café. And there they were, having arrived in the same moment!

And so they met in front of the door. From where he was standing Jean-Jacques had no way of seeing them, particularly since he was busy behind the counter, juggling multiple glasses between fingers made red by the cold water (he was economizing!) flowing from the tap. He was diligently washing and rinsing the glasses. As he did so, he kept his head lowered, his eyes fastened on the stream of water, and his mind, obviously, was somewhere else entirely. It was away with the fairies! He'd had yet another restless night, his sleep harrowed by unpleasant dreams. Elena had looked even older than in the previous dreams, emaciated, her skin more and more wrinkly, and the other woman, whom, for some unknown reason, he stubbornly insisted on calling Elvira, no longer came, she no longer set foot in his dreams. In vain did he continue to hope, when he awoke from the dream, soaked in sweat, and again closed his eyes, clenched his eyelids and fists, huddled tensely beneath the blankets and waited, in vain did he hope that maybe, just maybe the beautiful creature would appear once more, and here she was, good God, smiling from ear to ear, her white teeth gleaming like a string of pearls, here she was, in the flesh and blood, or in any case, swathed in fur, which she was now taking off, assisted by Yegor . . . Impossible! Impossible! It was too much!

Yegor hung the fur coat on the peg. After which he went up to the counter, with the bounding gait of a gymnast, and whispered something in the ear of Jean-Jacques, who was making an effort to control himself, to keep his cool: he listened, nodded, yes, of course, he'd serve her right away. Jean-Jacques didn't ask him the slightest question. He didn't dare, or rather he opened his mouth, moved his lips, but was unable to articulate a single word. Yegor didn't pay much attention, he turned around and with the same nonchalance went back to the table, where the woman had taken a book from her handbag and was flicking through it. Jean-Jacques filled two glasses with vodka, glasses somewhat larger than the ones in which vodka is usually served in Paris, and, his eyes slightly blurred, carried them over on a tray.

—Let me introduce you to Jean-Jacques, our beloved café proprietor, said Yegor.

The woman smiled and said nothing.

"What about her name?" thought Jean-Jacques, suspiciously. "What's her name? Is she called Elvira or Elena?" And Jean-Jacques all of a sudden felt like bursting into laughter. Not even he knew why. Nervous laughter, as they say. He managed to control himself, not to splutter with laughter, he transformed his laughter into a smile. And she too continued to smile. But also to remain silent. She raised her glass as if to make a toast and smiled even more broadly, at the same time furrowing her brow. She was looking at him with sweet eyes, at Jean-Jacques, who required no more than that to feel he was melting, liquefying. Then the woman decided to speak, to ask him a question:

—What kind of vodka is it, Russian?

She had a slightly husky voice and that highly distinctive accent, with a rough "r," rolling like a truck wheel over a badly asphalted highway.

—Yes, it's Russian vodka. All the way from Moscow.

—Usually they serve a Swedish brand. I'm not saying it's no good, but it's not really the same thing . . .

—Are you Russian? asked Jean-Jacques, plucking up courage, although he knew very well she couldn't be Russian; her accent wasn't at all Slavic.

Yegor stared in amazement; he rather overdid his amazement, his grimace. The woman looked at him and burst out laughing. She threw her head back and laughed, causing her breasts to jiggle up and down; she was chortling with laughter.

—Excuse me! said Jean-Jacques, who had seen one of his customers waving at him desperately, brandishing his newspaper, a copy of *Paris-Turf*. Excuse me, I have to go and . . .

—Go, and give a spin while you're at it, said Yegor in Russian, but Jean-Jacques didn't hear him, he was already at the table of the racetrack punter, who ordered a coffee, a cognac, and a packet of cigarettes, adding:

—She's beautiful, no denying it . . .

Jean-Jacques said nothing; he didn't linger to chat. He turned on his heel. Without looking he walked past the table where the two of them were cooing at each other in French; she spoke worse French than Yegor, who, the same as always when somebody else spoke worse French than him, was more than satisfied. He puffed up his feathers, like a turkey.

— . . . from Romania. From Moldavia, to be precise.

—From our Moldavia?

—No, from the Romanian Moldavia, from . . .

Jean-Jacques didn't catch the name, he couldn't hear it, because the racetrack punter, waiting to be served, shouted out the name of a horse which, in his opinion, could not but win.

—*Roman de gare*. It's a winning bet, a dead cert . . .

—I don't bet! . . . I don't bet anymore. I've lost too much money on horses in my time, muttered Jean-Jacques, hastily taking a tray to the customer's table. This was both true and not exactly true.

—Yes, but this time you can't lose. I guarantee.

—Bet on it yourself, if you're so sure!

—I'm betting on it, of course I am. I'm not ashamed to!

Yegor knocked back the rest of his drink and looked around for Jean-Jacques so that he could refill his glass.

—You'd think he was a prime minister with that name . . .

The woman shrugged.

—You don't speak any Russian at all?

—No . . . she sighed.

—A pity . . . Usually, Moldavians speak Russian too.

—But I'm from the Romanian Moldavia, from Romania, said the woman firmly, seeing that he was making out he didn't understand.

—We haven't even had time to tell each other our names, said Yegor presently and tried to touch her hand, but without success. Her hand gave a leap and hid next to the book. I see you're a keen reader, added the man and then called for Jean-Jacques. Jean-Jacques! What are you doing, man! Bring us some more vodka.

—Right away!

—My name is Yegor.

—Mine is Ana.

That evening, in bed, Yegor discovered much more about the beautiful Romanian than he had at the bar, where Jean-Jacques had been watching. After lovemaking, Ana seemed more relaxed than before. She lay with her arms beneath her neck, and with one leg bent, resting lightly on the other leg, as if she wished to conceal the furrow that Yegor had ploughed so diligently and productively. She answered the man's questions calmly, without haste. She'd been a doctor in Romania.

—What kind of doctor?

—What do you mean what kind?

—What was your speciality?

—I didn't have a speciality. I was a doctor in general . . . How do you say in French?

—*Médecin généraliste.*

Leaning on one elbow, the man looked at her with a kind of skeptical curiosity. She pretended not to notice his unbelieving, if not downright ironic, smile. Or perhaps she genuinely didn't notice it. She was talking and looking at the ceiling. She'd taken advantage of an invitation to a colloquium in Frankfurt. But she hadn't applied for asylum in Germany.

—Why not?

—I didn't like it there. In Germany there are no cities like Paris. Maybe Berlin, in the old days, but now that half of it's occupied by the Russians . . . Not that you see Russian soldiers there like you used to. They've left. But even so . . . It will take a while for it to get back to being the old Berlin again. Have you been to Berlin?

—No, I haven't.

—There, you see . . .

—Have you?

—No, I haven't. I told you already that I've been to Frankfurt . . .

—Then how do you know what it's like there?

—Where?

—In Berlin.

—From what I've heard . . .

In any case, she'd been dreaming of Paris ever since childhood. Her parents used to tell her about Paris, the Paris of their youth, between the wars. And so the groundwork had been laid. Then there was the language! She spoke French, but not German. She'd spoken French since she was a little child.

Yegor said something or other about having an accent.

—Never mind accent. We have the accent we have and that's that.

—The French have accents too, said Yegor, as if wishing to hearten her.

—What do you mean?

—Every region has a different accent.

—There, you see!

She spoke French with a Romanian accent. Although they'd lived in Paris for many years, her parents had an accent too. She picked up their accent. She didn't learn French in a French school, as her father would have liked. Nor did she learn it in Paris when she was a child. She didn't get the chance. The regime had changed, and her parents had lost everything they owned. Her father had also been sent to prison. To the Canal, the Romanian Gulag during the time of Gheorghiu-Dej, who was the head of the Party before Ceaușescu. Yes, her parents had been very rich, but the communists confiscated everything. They were left with a few precious items, a few pieces of jewelry that they'd managed to hide. Later they sold them one by one, to provide them with an income sufficient to let them eke out a living. The communists confiscated their house, but they continued to live in it as tenants. Except they no longer lived alone. They were forced to confine themselves to just a couple of rooms of their house, since they'd been forced to have another family move in with them, whose head was a man who had been put in charge of cadres at the factory where he'd once been an unqualified laborer. From time to time he'd get drunk and beat his wife and little boy, who couldn't have been more than five or six when the family moved in. Other than that, the head of cadres proved to be quite decent. In any event, he was better than others in the same situation. He didn't try to evict them so that he and his family could occupy the whole house. He even seemed to respect them. Anyhow, he gave the impression that the erstwhile owners intimidated him. He was probably aware of it himself. Of course he was! She burst out laughing: she was teaching her grandmother to suck eggs . . .

—But what did your parents do in Paris before the war? wondered Yegor.

—What did they do? They didn't do anything. They had fun.

Although very young, they were already married. They'd come to Paris for their honeymoon and, having stayed a month, they remained for the next few years. With brief interruptions. They returned to Romania from time to time, to their estate. When war broke out they were in Romania. They could have left the country very easily, but they didn't want to. For Romanians it was quite easy to travel during the war; they were allied with the Germans, after all. But her parents didn't feel like leaving the country in the middle of a war. They'd have been accused of who knows what. True, her father was exempted from army service, but tongues would still have wagged. The people they knew in Paris insisted that they return; life wasn't all that bad in France. Granted, the country was occupied, but people who were well-off managed, as did those who were later to be denounced as collaborators. Some even had a whale of a time. Her parents had friends in Paris, important people, including that writer who had been ambassador to Romania . . . What was his name?[1]

Yegor didn't know what his name was. He got up from the bed and put on his long johns, shirt, trousers.

—Are you getting dressed?

In the woman's voice regret manifested itself almost as a reproach.

—I've got things to do, said Yegor and started looking for his socks. Under the bed. On all fours. He swept the parquet with his arm and encountered an object which, once brought to light, proved to be a small tape recorder, a very small one, the size of a matchbox.

—What's this?

—What does it look like? A Dictaphone.

—So small?

The woman tried to continue her story about her parents, but the man was no longer listening. He was fiddling with the tape recorder. In fact he was trying to turn it on and to see whether it had recorded anything.

1 Paul Morand (1888–1976)—*Translator's note.*

—It's broken, she said.

—Probably. Anyhow, it doesn't have a tape.

—That may be . . .

—What was it doing under the bed?

—Must have fallen . . .

—It fell there by itself?

—The law of gravity!

—Merci. And was it the law of gravity that pushed it all the way back?

Ana was bored of the interrogation. She sat up. In any event, there was nothing else left to do in bed. The man seemed determined to abandon the battlefield for the time being.

As a child she'd fallen in love with a cockerel. At least that's what her mother told her later, laughing. She'd have liked to take it to bed with her at night, but was unable to, for obvious reasons. Then they bought her a toy cockerel, a stuffed one. It was dear to her . . . She used to fall asleep with it in her arms.

Jean-Jacques no longer needed to point out that the table by the coatrack was reserved: nobody dared sit down there. If a newcomer entered the café and happened to go to the table in question, the other customers, the regulars, would make vigorous signs to dissuade him, waving a finger or hand: no, not there! The newcomer wouldn't understand why, but wouldn't insist, particularly given that there were plenty of vacant tables. He'd shrug and sit down somewhere else.

One fine morning, in came Yegor, who, instead of going to the bar, muttering a *bonjour*, leaning his elbows on the counter, and looking fixedly at Jean-Jacques as he waited to be served, went straight to the reserved table and, taking no notice of the others' hand-waving, pulled out a chair and sat down. Silence fell in the café. With baited breath, everybody was waiting for the barman to react. With the utmost slowness, the barman moved the glass he was rinsing under the stream of water, carefully turned off the faucet, looked at Yegor, and shook his head. He slowly came out from behind the counter. He coughed two or three times, covering his mouth and chin with his hand. With leisurely gait, he walked over to the table at which sat the man whom he'd been in the habit of regarding as more or less a friend. The customers at more distant tables half stood up, propping themselves with their arms on the tabletops, and then they rose to their feet, the better to watch the scene. Some took a few steps forward. Others craned their necks, stood on tiptoes.

Jean-Jacques came to a stop next to Yegor, folded his arms across his chest, and waited. In the café the silence had become deafening. Each customer could hear his heart thudding. Without losing his cool in the slightest, Yegor curtly uttered the words:

—A vodka.

Jean-Jacques looked at him for a few seconds, unfolded his arms and jerked his shoulders, stooping as if disburdening himself. Then he turned on his heel. At the bar, his gestures were the same as ever, the ones he'd repeated tens of thousands of times. He filled a glass with vodka. He placed it on a tray. With measured steps he went back to Yegor's table. After serving him without so much as a single word, Jean-Jacques returned to the bar. The customers sat back down. Some turned their heads to look elsewhere, preferably outside, at the street, although the street was barely visible because of the window, which hadn't been washed for centuries . . .

"Life is simple," Yegor thought, proud of himself, and lit a cigarette. After looking around himself triumphantly, he rummaged in his pocket and pulled out rather a small newspaper, printed in Cyrillic script. He unfolded it with a look of satisfaction.

Jean-Jacques sighed and set about washing the glasses he'd washed once already. He thought that just maybe his friend was being a braggart. But then he looked at him more closely—he was no longer reading the newspaper, he'd folded it back up and placed it between the ashtray and his glass of vodka—and he realized that Yegor was in a good mood, what was more, his entire being radiated if not happiness, then at least contentment. He was smoking with his head thrown back, blowing smoke rings at the ceiling.

She liked to skip a rope. Especially when she was wearing the blue dress that was her favorite. Maybe because that was what she was wearing when her father once photographed her skipping. They were in Maramureş, in a village at the foot of some rather tall hills, almost miniature mountains. She was skipping between some flower and vegetable beds, and her father, hiding behind a plum tree, with his camera, of which he was very proud—it's a German make!—was trying to photograph her mid-jump. What he was trying to do was by no means simple. He wasted an entire roll of film in order finally to get a single photograph: Ana in mid-air, her knees bent. Far in the background could be seen the beautifully carved wooden gate of a farmhouse, and up above, to the right, there was a strange animal, which couldn't be a fish, although that was what it looked like, but most likely it was a bird captured mid-flight by the German camera.

Yegor climbed the stairs of a bourgeois building where well-off, if not wealthy people must have lived. There was, of course, an elevator, which worked impeccably—a very tall, slightly balding man had just emerged from the cabin, smoothing the collar of his raincoat with the back of his hand—but Yegor preferred to climb the stairs to the sixth floor, without haste. No, he wasn't claustrophobic. Rather, he wanted to draw out the time, to delay. Ana attracted him, but at the same time she somehow made him afraid. She intimidated him. Perhaps this is what needs to be said . . . She intimidated him and stirred doubts in him. How so, doubts? I can't quite put my finger on it: just doubts. In the first place, how was it that she lived in such an expensive building? And in such a chic neighborhood. Even if her apartment was small and quite modestly furnished . . . The rent must have been huge. How could she afford it? After all the things that had happened in the East, it was very hard, if not impossible, to obtain political asylum. She'd have had to demonstrate that despite the change of regime, her freedom was imperilled. Let's say that she'd already obtained political asylum and with it benefit payments, but even so, such benefits would be meagre to say the least. As well as very difficult to carry on claiming under the new circumstances. Then she must have found a job. Where? When? She didn't look like the kind of person who had a job. Not even the most insignificant job. How then did she manage? What did she live on? Where did she get the money?

In the end he wasn't brave enough to ask her. What right had he to subject her to an interrogation? He of all people, who hated being asked too many questions. It was a throwback from Russia, where, as a student, he'd gone through a rather troubled period, which he didn't like to recall. He of all people, harassing her like that! He felt guilty about the feeling of suspicion he harbored toward that mysterious, beautiful woman, but his curiosity wouldn't die down. Quite the opposite: after he found that tape recorder under the bed, his suspicion only increased. You might say it became a genuine obsession. No matter what he did, it was the only thing he thought about! He'd even been on the verge of confessing everything to Jean-Jacques and asking him for his advice. But he didn't. He changed his mind at the last moment. Jean-Jacques was a strange, closed sort of person. Rarely did he talk about himself. Anyhow, he wasn't the man most suited to hear such a confession. Besides, Yegor would also have had to confess his passionate, carnal relationship with Ana, the woman Jean-Jacques gave the impression of liking very strongly. Sure, the barman suspected what was going on . . . When he saw him the other day sitting at the table reserved for

Ana, what a dark look he'd given him! He controlled himself, but he was probably really jealous. He himself was in a similar sort of situation. Maybe in his case too all his suspicions were in fact down to simple jealousy. Although he had no tangible motives to be jealous. Anyhow, he had fewer motives than Jean-Jacques. The tape recorder? Well, for a start, it was broken . . . After all, why should he get het up about a device that has become commonplace? Everybody has one! And what was more, he couldn't find any explanation, he couldn't see, for example, any connection between the recording device and the eventuality that Ana might be entertaining another man in her bed. It was pure jealousy, which is to say, it wasn't supported by any remotely concrete or coherent scenario. He had only another floor to climb and he was still far from unravelling the enigma. He felt his pocket, inside which there was a bottle of Russian vodka all the way from Russia. God, why was everything so complicated! It was further complicated by his impression that Ana herself felt a need that he should ask her all kinds of questions. Really? Yes, as if otherwise she couldn't have existed in the other person's eyes, as if otherwise she'd have been nothing but a shadow, an outline glimpsed in a café, and then a beautiful woman you sleep with and that's all: *une poupée gonflable*, an inflatable doll. She herself needed his questions. Ultimately, it was almost unimportant whether the questions were provoked by jealousy, by suspicion, rather than by a desire to get to know the person dear to him better. Sure, to ask her questions in order to get to know her better would be ideal and there was no point in him protesting from pure hypocrisy or just for her sake. Maybe *hypocrisy* wasn't the right word. He couldn't find one more appropriate. But he understood very well what it was all about . . .

Spring was on its way. It was still late February, but for two or three days it had been so warm that it was no surprise that the trees had started to bud. It wasn't a good thing, thought

Ana, suddenly concerned about what would become of nature. What if a frost arrived to nip the buds! As it was warm, she was wearing just her trench coat. Underneath she had on a miniskirt and a very close-fitting sleeveless blouse. She stood leaning against a lamppost. Passing men looked at her, some smiled at her, but they didn't stop. She almost felt insulted. After a while she shrugged and set off for the Métro station.

A few days later, Ana tried to explain to the man lying next to her why it was necessary to talk afterwards. Post-coital conversations! Yegor stroked his pectoral muscles and for a time, for a good few minutes, he asked no further questions, he kept shtum. He was thinking of something else. Of another woman? Or of the bottle of vodka on the nightstand, on which Ana had placed two rather large glasses: she knew her lover couldn't stand small glasses. In the glasses on the nightstand—if not in both, then at least in one of them—there was still a little vodka, but he grabbed the bottle and took a long swig from it. Then, abruptly:

—What about your father?

—You haven't understood . . . Father died first. He can't have been even sixty years old. I don't know how old he was exactly.

—Was he ill?

—Ill? Hardly! He was as healthy as an ox . . . After all the persecution he'd suffered, the years in prison, the humiliation, the hunger, there wasn't a thing wrong with him. "You'll live to attend the funerals of every one of us!" Mother used to say, who was obsessed with the idea of death. I don't know why, because at the time she wasn't ill. Maybe it was a kind of presentiment. Because she did fall ill not long after Father's death. Ever since I knew her or ever since I was first able to understand what she was saying, she'd talked about death at every opportunity. For a while I believed that she wanted to draw attention to herself, but it wasn't like that; she quite simply couldn't stop herself. She used to annoy my father with that morbid obsession of hers.

"Stop moaning all the time!" he used to say. She didn't even protest. Only now do I realize that death for her was a real obsession. Although she was younger than Father. Five or so years younger . . . Or four . . . I can't remember!

—What was the cause of death?

—Whose? Mother's?

—No, your father's . . .

—He liked to roam around the country. "Here today, tomorrow in Focșani!" That's what he used to say, and he'd whistle. "Don't whistle in the house," Mother would say, "whistling indoors brings bad luck . . ." "You don't say." And he'd whistle all the more. "It's because you don't let me go out. At least let me wander around the country. Around the homeland! It belongs to me, too, not just to the communists!" He had a big mouth. That's why they locked him up . . . He used to say whatever he liked. The regime was very harsh in those years. In the end he mellowed. Little by little . . .

—Was he locked up for a long time?

—Two or three years. Not long. When he was released, he didn't seem changed at all. Maybe he was a little thinner. And he had more friends.

—Had he made them in prison?

—I don't know. In that village on the Danube where he was assigned obligatory domicile. The fact is, I don't know how he made all those friends or what he was mixed up in to be invited to visit all kinds of places. He knew all the small towns in the provinces. "All the back-of-beyond places . . ." as Mother used to grumble. "I've got friends," he'd say. "Drinking buddies," Mother would retort. Sometimes he took her with him. Maybe he'd have taken her more often, if it had been up to him. I don't know . . . He liked to travel alone, not to have to have anybody in tow. He'd pack his suitcase the night before, get up at the crack of dawn, and go to the station to catch the train. True, we lived very close to Bucharest's Northern Station. Just a few streets away. When he came back, he sometimes brought a painting in his suitcase. Landscapes, portraits . . .

—Did he paint them?

—I don't think so. I never saw him painting at home. He had friends who were painters. Once he brought home a portrait of a woman. Mother looked at it; she was furious. She said the name of a woman, which I don't recall, and then she stormed out of the living room, slamming the door behind her.

—Maybe he had a mistress . . .

—Maybe, but I don't think so. He wasn't the type! I rather think that he liked to chew the fat over a glass of wine.

—Did he tipple?

—No . . . You couldn't say that. He liked to talk, sometimes to criticize the government. Or rather the regime . . . "That lot!" as he used to say.

—Wasn't he afraid? He'd been in trouble because of it before . . .

—No. He used to say that he couldn't care less. It's true that the times had changed. Nobody got locked up for idle talk anymore. That was what happened under Stalinism, when the regime had to strike dread into people no matter what. Into the bourgeoisie! In the Gheorghiu-Dej period, in other words. In the final years, you didn't even get locked up for political jokes anymore. Do you know the story about the poet who was shouting "Down with Ceaușescu!" in the street and the police were reluctant to arrest him? It was late at night, after midnight, and the poet was drunk out of his mind. The policemen followed him, tried to persuade him to shut up, to calm down, they threatened him, shoved him . . . To no effect! In the end they arrested him, because they didn't have any choice, but they released him the next day. After the chairman of the Writers Union intervened. True, the poet was drunk . . . Somebody else—not a poet, an engineer—pasted up posters instigating a rebellion. Granted, him they caught. They arrested him, threw him in the slammer.

He had a dire time of it . . . On his behalf nobody intervened. Apparently he died under torture.

—Then where did he get the paintings? Did he buy them?

—No, I don't think so. As I told you, he had friends. All kinds of friends . . . They probably included painters too. But sometimes maybe he bought the paintings . . .

—Yes, yes . . . And then what? You still haven't told me how your father died.

—He died suddenly!

—A car accident?

—An accident, yes, but not a car accident. He died asphyxiated by a gas stove. He was gassed!

—How was that?

—He was visiting a friend in the country, who put him up in a barn recently converted into a cottage for guests. People had stayed in it before, but only in summer. Father arrived in late autumn. It was cold. A region where the cheapest and simplest way of keeping warm was gas. I'm not really sure why the chimney was completely blocked. Apparently a stork had made a nest on top of the chimney. The stork and the chicks had departed, but the nest remained. Because of the nest, Father departed too. Permanently. The gas, or rather the combusted gas, instead of going up the chimney, spread through the room, filled Father's lungs. Slowly but surely. He died in his sleep.

—Didn't he smell anything?

—Nothing. Otherwise he'd have gotten up, gone out of the room. Or at least he'd have dragged himself to the door, tried to breathe through the crack at the bottom.

—He didn't suffer . . .

—Apparently you don't. It's the same as with anesthesia.

—You don't suffer and you're not afraid. That's even better . . .

—Mother had no such luck! Mother was wracked by cancer for a long time. She suffered. It was horrible . . . She didn't want to die. She wanted to live. No matter what. She became a kind of wild animal, struggling in the claws of death. She couldn't bear to have anybody around her. She had a grudge against me in particular. I don't know why. She said that she should have stayed in Paris. That she shouldn't have listened to my father, who was dead set on returning to Romania. As if people don't die of cancer in Paris too. They die of it in droves here in Paris too! "But I got cancer in Romania, in this shithole of a country!" she'd yell. As you can imagine, she wasn't afraid of anything anymore. In the hospital she used to hurl abuse at everybody. They were all guilty because she was dying. Ceaușescu more than anyone else. She had an especial grudge against the dictator's wife, Elena. She constantly called her a whore. A whore, a scorpion, and other such endearments. The doctors were at their wits' end. They drugged her. They pumped her full of morphine. I think they were increasing her dose every day. By the end, I mean. It might be argued that they euthanized her. True, there was nothing else they could do for her.

—Did she believe in God?

—I don't think so . . . She didn't believe in anything. Maybe only in the devil.

—Same thing. If you believe in the devil, logically speaking, you also have to believe in God, decided Yegor and took another swig straight from the bottle.

—Is that your opinion? Why don't you use a glass?

—Yes, that's my opinion . . . It's better from the bottle.

—Drink from the bottle then. Nobody's stopping you . . .

—Before she died, did you summon a priest?

—A priest?

—Yes, a priest! What's so amazing about that? It's supposed to be the done thing . . .

—She died in hospital. And in a Ceaușescu-era hospital it was hard to summon a priest. I hope you understand . . .

—But was she baptized? Orthodox? and here he grabbed the bottle again.

—I don't know. How should I know? I didn't attend her baptism. But I think about how, if she'd believed in God, maybe she wouldn't have suffered so much . . .

—Maybe you're right, said Yegor and took another swig.

—Don't drink it all yourself. Give me a sip too!

They drank the whole bottle. Ultimately, it was quite small. Yegor didn't sleep over. He never did, in fact. Even if after love-making—after lovemaking and vodka—he happened to nod off, he'd soon wake up, get dressed, and leave. True, Ana seldom suggested that he stay. And even when she did, it was half-heartedly. Was she afraid that Mihai might telephone? Anything is possible . . . This is why, if she saw there was a risk that he might fall fast asleep, she'd fidget, move about the room making all kinds of noises, picking things up, dropping them, in short, she made sure he'd wake up. Probably she preferred to sleep alone too. Real celibates. Both of them.

He didn't like to recall his student years in Moscow, where he'd gone to study foreign languages—French to be precise—moving to the capital from a nearby small town.

—Why do you want to study French? a scrawny man had asked him suspiciously, having popped up as if from the ground shortly after the start of the academic year.

Yegor mumbled something about literature, the need to translate European literature in order to maintain contact with progressive writers from over there . . . This wasn't what his interlocutor was interested in; he'd been assigned the specific task of recruitment to a certain important organization. He'd picked out Yegor precisely because he was a provincial and looked slightly addled. The fact that he didn't really understand what it was all about seemed to amuse the other man and motivate him all the more. What about his fellow students? What was it that prompted them to learn foreign languages? Yegor shrugged. How should he know . . .

—Our state needs speakers of foreign languages . . . People we can send to France, Germany, the States . . .

Yegor still didn't get it. He agreed with everything the KGB man said, and when it came to signing, he signed. Only then did he understand. But he signed. That was the truth: he signed . . .

—Who is Mihai? Johannes or perhaps Dieter asked her one evening.

—We went to the same lyceum . . . But why?

—He telephoned, asked to speak to you.

—When?

—A couple of hours ago.

—What did he say? Is he going to call back?

—I don't know, he didn't say. He apologized and hung up.

It wasn't what might be called a door; it wasn't even a curtain that might be moved aside. It was rather a blotch of color or a light, a red, glaring light. He hesitated for a moment or two and then rushed at it headfirst, he threw himself into the light, hoping that beyond it she'd be waiting, stretched out on the silver fox fur, naked, welcoming. Burning. Jean-Jacques therefore ripped through the redness that took the place of a door, and when he found Ana before him he abruptly came to a stop. Ana stretched out her arms to him, smiled at him. Encouragingly. Enticingly.

This happened immediately after he found out what her name was. Yegor had told him her name one fine morning. He entered the café in a hurry and went straight to the bar. Propping himself on his elbows, he ordered a glass of vodka, and then another. He knocked both glasses back in one gulp. The naturalness with which he did this almost had a powerful effect on those who witnessed it. Yegor hadn't the slightest hesitation when he raised the glass to his lips. He drank like a thirsty man. He never winced after swallowing the drink. His throat was inured to vodka. It was like a tanned hide, you might say.

He experienced the real sensation of well-being in the moment when the vodka reached his stomach and spread its beneficent warmth . . . It's no wonder that the hand holding the glass stretched out to the barman once again. Almost automatically.

—Is she Romanian? Jean-Jacques asked him once more.

Yegor didn't answer immediately this time either. First he knocked back the small glass of vodka that Jean-Jacques had filled in a trice and banged it back down on the counter with a gesture signifying that he wanted another and had no inclination to wait. Jean-Jacques didn't even flinch; he grabbed the bottle and poured the fourth, if not fifth, glass of the morning.

—Tell me!

—Yes, she's Romanian and her name's Ana. At least that's how she introduced herself, said Yegor and raised his glass with a movement slower than hitherto.

—Hannah?

—Yes, Ana, Anne, in your language. Which lends itself to a rather bizarre homophony . . .

Jean-Jacques didn't pick up on the aggression in Yegor's tone and words. Maybe he didn't even understand what he meant about homophony. He didn't understand that Yegor had no way of distinguishing between long and short vowels. Or else he pretended not to understand . . . Maybe he was thinking that it was a pity her name wasn't Elvire. Or rather Elvira, since she was Romanian after all . . . Obviously, Ana is a Romanian name too. Or an Italian one. Probably more Romanian than . . . But he'd got used to the name Elvira. It reminded him of the actress. Of Elvire Popesco, when she was younger . . . The Russian had no way of knowing; he hadn't seen the actress when she was younger. He'd show him a photograph of her. Even in the photograph she looked like Ana: as alike as two drops of water.

—Or vodka, said Yegor.

—Another glass?

—No, I'd better eat something. Make me an omelette, he

added in his Slavic-accented French and sat down at a table. With a tomato on the side. I'm quite hungry. When you bring me the omelette, you can pour me another glass. In fact, you can pour me it now, since I'm hardly likely to get drunk on so little . . .

—I wasn't worried that you would!

—See, that's what I like about you, muttered Yegor in satisfaction.

—With cheese or ham?

—With mushrooms . . .

This time, he refrained from sitting at her table. Jean-Jacques smiled at him gratefully and hurried off to the kitchen. He almost trod on the fish that was hiding by the door. He merely brushed it with the tip of his boot, but he didn't see it or feel it against his foot.

The hair is blond, reddish-blond, Venetian. The forehead is neither too broad nor too bulbous. The features, which are regular, might be described as ordinary. True, in order to be accepted without too much cavilling, beauty ought to be ordinary more than anything else. Lest it shock. That it might seep almost imperceptibly into the beholder's awareness, that it might match every taste to a greater or lesser degree. That it might be eligible, that it might even indulge in a little demagoguery . . .

Maybe the painter avoided emphasizing the face. Obviously it was difficult for him to ignore it, as long as he claimed to be painting a portrait; but what seemed to have interested him more than the woman's face was her bust, to be more precise, her generous cleavage, in which he added a lot of white and pink. Or maybe it wasn't even the cleavage . . . Maybe it's simply the abstract pattern of the blouse that's the true subject of the painting . . .

She hadn't applied for political asylum in Germany, even though there she'd have been able to practice medicine without breaking the law, since a Romanian qualification was recognized, accepted. In France it isn't possible. The laws are very strict, aimed at protecting the French university system and the doctors it produces. Did she not know that? Did she really not know? Everybody knew, that is, all the doctors from Romania and other East European states must have known, otherwise they'd all have come here in droves. You understand? And Yegor looked at her mistrustfully. She shook her head. In denial. Anyhow, when she decided to remain in the West, she didn't pause to think very hard about the consequences. She left the colloquium, went to the train station and bought a ticket to Paris . . .

—Did you also have a visa for France?

—I didn't. I declared at the border that I wanted to claim political asylum.

—And the German border guards let you pass? Didn't they question you? What about the French?

—Yes, they did. But they were quite confused themselves about what was happening in the East. Probably they didn't have any clear instructions.

—But what language did you talk to them in?

—In English.

—You speak English?

—A little. I learned in lyceum. How good do you think a border guard's English can be?

—Good enough. Anyhow, he can get by. As long as he's not French.

—What do you mean?

—Because the French aren't capable of learning a foreign language. Because of their accent, the tonic accent, which is fixed in French.

—You're exaggerating! And how do you know all this?

—I know. I've read about it. For the Germans, for example, it seems it's much easier: they have a mobile tonic accent, the same as the English. Not to mention that the two languages are related . . . They're first cousins.

In that moment Yegor remembered that the first time he saw her in the café she had been reading a book in German. He couldn't remember the title. In fact, it wasn't he himself who saw the book, but Jean-Jacques, who may have been mistaken; maybe it wasn't in German. And so he decided against asking her about it. She could have answered anything at all, for example she could have claimed that she was reading a book about musical theory. He'd seen a number of books of that kind in the small bookcase ornamented with elephants in the corner of the room, which gave the impression of being a small salon. They were not in German, it was true, although one of them was about Johann Sebastian Bach and the art of the fugue. But could he be sure? He'd seen it only in passing. He promised himself that at the first opportunity he'd examine the books in the bookcase more carefully. He was a librarian, after all. In any case, that was what he had told her, in answer to her idle question, asked without insistence.

—Really? You're a librarian? Where?

—At the arrondissement library, he replied, without going into further detail.

Nor did Ana ask him to go into detail. Her gaze slid down toward the man's member, which seemed to be emerging from quiescence, even to be signalling its presence through a discreet and gradual augmentation of volume. But the man was still in the mood for conversation. And because the conversation was underway and the awkward subject had been broached without too much embarrassment on either the one side or the other, Yegor ventured to ask her how she spent her time when she wasn't at the café or in bed with him. And she gave a slightly whinnying laugh. Ana then laid her thigh over his thigh and his member, as if about to mount him, and plugged his mouth with hers. That meant she was sick of questions and would have preferred that they both occupy themselves with something completely different. Yegor could not but agree with her. He clasped her in his arms and, with a shove, reversed the situation in his favor. Actually, that can't be said with complete certainty . . . In the first place, because the man's physical and mental effort was more intense than that of his partner, who, at least at first, didn't seem to be putting much heart into it, quite the contrary, her right arm had stretched out to an almost unnatural length and her hand was groping for something under the bed. Yegor didn't notice anything. His eyes were closed, perhaps so that he could concentrate better and coordinate more accurately the movements of his pelvis, thighs and, at the same time, head, lips, and tongue, a highly complex gymnastic number, of which Ana took advantage without making any great input. A few minutes later, after the arm and hand had found what they were looking for and the fingers had pressed the button of the small device, her interest in the man busy on top of her, with his panting and rather noisy chomping, her interest, if we might put it like that, intensified and turned into pleasure, and so this time it would be possible to speak of genuine participation on her part, which by no means facilitated the male's task, quite the contrary, the demands of the entire enterprise increased markedly, the bed was creaking from every joint, the pleasure was rising like a tide that would drown both of them at about the same time.

It was still too early. A single customer had shown up; he gave the impression of someone unsuccessfully trying to come round from a hangover. He asked for a double espresso and sat down at the table farthest to the back. Jean-Jacques served him without making any remark. He then absorbed himself in reading a copy of the *Nouvel Observateur* left behind by a customer a few days earlier.

He came across an interesting article. It was about the hell endured by numerous women from the East who, as soon as the door to the West had opened a crack, had swarmed to the capitalist paradise. "Sequestered, beaten, thrown onto the street, forced to prostitute themselves: 120,000 women from the East have fallen into the snares of the sex traffickers in less than two years." The reporter had chosen to focus on the story of one of the women, from the town of Roman in Moldavia. On the two years of misery endured by this woman in her thirties, who had been lured by the mirage of the West. Leaving her native town, near the border with the Republic of Moldova, Aneta had crossed Romania by bus and entered Yugoslavia, her ticket having been paid for by the "organizers." Near Sarajevo, the "nice organizers" had turned into brutes. Aneta had found herself without papers or money, forced to work for a few weeks in a nightclub, where she served at the bar and waited tables. She was too plump to be a stripper, and so in the end she was sold to an Albanian. For five thousand dollars. Her life now became a genuine hell. Sequestered in an apartment in Tirana, she and another Moldavian woman were forced to prostitute themselves for almost a year. Day after day, for hours on end . . .

Luckily for her, one fine day her owner decided to send her to Italy, where she could earn him a lot more money as a streetwalker. The coast of the Italian peninsula is guarded day and night. Together with some other women, Aneta crossed the Adriatic on a motorboat, a Zodiac. The craft sank somewhere off the coast of Puglia. Soaking wet, shivering with cold, Aneta and the other women waited in a forest for the truck to take them to Milan, Rome, or Turin. But instead of a truck, the Carabinieri turned up and took them to a special center in Santa Foca. Funded by the Italian state and run by a priest, Don Cesare Lo Deserto, the center spelled salvation for Aneta and the other women in her situation. The article ended with the romance between the Romanian woman and Achimil, a young Iraqi migrant, who worked under the direct supervision of Don Cesare.

Jean-Jacques broke off reading the article. A number of people had entered the café and were impatient to consume their morning coffee and croissant.

The beautiful Ana of course had a host of admirers among the habitués of the café. One of them was the assiduous reader of the racing press, from which he was never parted. Or almost never, since, returning from the track, from Auteuil or Longchamp, after an unlucky day, he obviously sometimes threw away in disgust the newspaper he'd pored over fruitlessly the whole morning, at home or in the café. He'd throw it away in a fury, although after that he'd go and buy another copy, because he was an incorrigible collector, horse racing was an object of study for him, not merely another form of entertainment, as it was for most of the people who went to the track.

One such day, after he'd thrown his newspaper away and was slowly walking through the Bois de Boulogne, looking right and left, he thought he saw the woman from the café. She was wearing her usual outfit, which is to say, under the silver fox fur she can't have had much on. She'd climbed out of a car and was probably waiting for another silver fox fur enthusiast to drive up. She was staring into space, the way she did in the café when she wasn't reading. He was therefore able to examine closely, from just three or four meters, that rictus of hers, which betokened suffering or, perhaps, the suppression of unbearable memories. Granted, he could have examined it in the café too, and here it was harder . . . To do so our gambling man would have had to position himself somewhere not too far away, perhaps even to hide behind a tree, in order to get a good long look at her. Or else he'd have had to walk up to her without hesitation, try to strike up a conversation. Broke as he was, he didn't even dare look at her too insistently, let alone talk to her. And so he went his way, merely slowing his steps a little.

But could he be mistaken? Might he be hallucinating? Was he certain that the woman in the Bois de Boulogne was one and the same person as the woman he saw almost every day in the café? The woman who read avidly, without looking around her, all kinds of German and English books, thick, serious books, which impressed the reader of *Paris-Turf* and made him doubt what he'd seen in the Bois de Boulogne. No, it couldn't be she, even if the woman on the path looked like her and wore a silver fox fur the same as she did. It was merely a coincidence. Fur coats look alike. Women, too. Especially when they're beautiful.

Johannes was on his knees, next to her body, which was stretched facedown and abandoned to his whims. They were naked, naturally, both the one and the other. They uttered not a word. In his left hand the man was holding a jar, in which could be seen a reddish-yellow substance, similar to honey. Perhaps it really was honey . . . From time to time, he tipped the jar and poured some of the semi-liquid substance into his cupped hand and then carefully applied it to the woman's back, to the middle of her back, to be precise, along the spinal column. His gestures were slow, exaggeratedly slow; you would've thought it was a monotonous ritual. But the woman didn't seem to react in any way. She lay inert. And the man was very absorbed, but no more than that: he was neither moved nor excited. It was obvious that he wasn't making those gestures for the first time. The scene unfolded without surprises, without untoward incident.

When she was little, she used to clamber on top of her father and bite him on the nose. It was a game of theirs. Probably at first she just kissed him on the nose. In order to avoid his mouth, which smelled of tobacco. And not only tobacco . . . And so she preferred to kiss him on the nose. He had a prominent nose. In jest, she went from kisses to bites. Her mother was appalled by it. Especially since her father seemed to like it. At least that was what was in Sofica's head. That's what her mother was called. Her father used to protest and pretend that it hurt. Little Ana would swoop on his nose, which was as large as a potato and rather ruddy—a drunkard's nose, as his wife said—and stroke it, bite it, suck it. Sofica was convinced that George found pleasure in that rough and tumble. And not a paternal, innocent pleasure. What about the little girl? In any case, little Ana was getting cheekier and cheekier, especially toward her mother, who was rather stern. Perhaps too stern . . .

—You're to blame, you gave her your nose!

—Why do you always have to exaggerate! her father said, defensively.

Sofica shrugged and went into another room. She wasn't quite as indignant as she wished to appear. She'd pick up a book and read. Or she'd turn on the radio. In Romania there were no televisions yet.

—What year was it?

Ana didn't answer that indiscreet question. He may well think himself sly, but it wouldn't work with her. She changed the subject. Yegor went back on the attack. For a start, how could she have memories from such a tender age? No matter how strongly such and such an event may have affected her. And there was no way that episode with the nose could have been an event even for such a precocious little girl as she must have been. Certainly, little girls are more precocious than little boys. It's well known! The species needs, or rather needed, the female sex to develop more quickly, that is, earlier: to be capable of reproduction.

Ana tittered. Memories? They weren't genuine memories, they were reconstructions, she explained. Scenes that she reconstructed with the help of her mother. They were her mother's memories, not hers. She merely adopted them. And in time they probably altered slightly in her mind.

—Childhood is like a dream, murmured Yegor.

Ana blew a raspberry.

—It depends what you mean by childhood. You don't remember much about the first three or four years. Not even as much as you remember from a dream.

—Because you suppress it . . .

—You know what? Don't give me any of your two-bit Freudianism. Memory is in any case something atrocious. The effort of remembering is pointless. Deleterious even . . . Alzheimer's, which is found only in humans, is manna from heaven: it helps you accept the ultimate outcome . . . Better not to know where you are or what's happening to you! Maybe it's even triggered by the fear of death, which is specific to humans and which you would say was stupid if it weren't so deeply rooted in everybody. Anyway, rationality stands no chance of opposing it . . .

Yegor looked at her not knowing what to believe. He cleared his throat. He wanted to say something, but thought better of it. Look at how fearful she is! It never even crossed his mind that he had the honor of being in bed with a philosopher.

She spent hours on end grooming her legs. Particularly her feet, which she found loathsome, ugly: knobbly and callused. When she was younger she never took off her stockings or socks in front of a man. To the Japanese, this is a sign of great refinement, she claimed and, in regard to socks, it was the truth. The men she made love to didn't get hung up on this detail. But it annoyed her to have such broad, knobbly feet. She'd look at them now with pity, now with scorn. She knew very well that there wasn't a great deal she could do about it. Even if she'd kept them wrapped in cotton wool, she still wouldn't have been able to ameliorate the problem to any great extent. True, overly tight footwear aggravated the problem, and this is how the calluses had formed. She waged war against them, going to see a pedicurist, although nor was he able to perform miracles.

Gradually, she began to become accustomed to her own feet. Particularly since the legs, the calves and the thighs, were nothing to be sniffed at. After a while, she said to herself that men don't even look at your feet, they form a view of the whole and excitement prevents them from examining the details. But what about afterwards? After the sexual act, in the transition period, when the two partners are waiting for the male to regain his strength and set to work once more? It's those moments that are the most dangerous, from every point of view. For both partners. It's then that they see each other's flaws. This was why Ana became talkative and tried to draw the man's attention to a higher level, she forced him, in other words, to look her in the eyes. In time, however, she realized that she had nothing to fear. Neither Mihai nor Yegor let their eyes travel down to her feet, and even if they did, they didn't seem shocked in the slightest at what they saw. Johannes was the only one who seemed vaguely repulsed by her feet. Obviously, the German was a special case. For him, the excitement was intellectual and aesthetic rather than sexual. Not that he let slip any insulting remark, no matter how small, he wasn't taken aback, he didn't look at her feet closely. Rather he seemed to avoid looking at them. One evening, she was even on the verge of telling him, in jest: "Why don't you anoint my feet with honey . . ." But she refrained.

At that time of day the Métro was swarming. In such circumstances, the disparity between the two categories of passenger is all the more striking: those seated nicely and those condemned to stand. It's difficult to move from one category to another. Those seated nicely give the impression that they'd rather stay on the train to the end of the line than stand up and relinquish their coveted seats to one of those standing. The eyes of the latter brim with hatred and desire. The cohabitation of these two feelings may sometimes be termed hope. This is because there's no word to denote the feeling that goes with the condition of waiting. Indeed, everybody is waiting. Some look at their watches every two minutes, others look for the umpteenth time at the advertisements, which lately have been replaced by posters featuring short and rather dopey poems. But even so, they're better than nothing! Those standing know them almost by heart. Those seated are further privileged in this respect too. They're not obliged to read the advertisements or the poems selected by the refined functionaries in the employ of the RATP. They bring with them books or newspapers to their own taste and read them with delectation. The women, most of all, but sometimes even the men. Sticklers will claim that the seated merely pretend to read, in order thereby to avoid the reproachful eyes of those standing. And the latter close their eyes from time to time, having wearied of constant coveting. In their pockets, briefcases, and handbags they too have books or newspapers, proof that the miracle of moving from one category to another can occur at any time. Take that little old man, for example, probably a pensioner, who has no business riding the Métro during rush hour, look at him folding up the newspaper he's been reading and getting ready to stand up. His hesitant movements are rather unsettling, and the other privileged sitters look at him somewhat reproachfully. Such an abrupt abandonment of a seat is a kind of betrayal! His intention also disturbs those standing, since only one of them will benefit. The old man mumbles words of apology, with a great effort he wrenches himself from his seat, tries to advance, the train pulls into a station, other passengers push their way aboard, and our pensioner finds that he can no longer alight, since the doors have closed in his face. He doesn't seem very put out. Probably he foresaw this failure or else he merely wanted to get off at the next station. Now he's by the doors, crowded, crushed, but it's certain that he will be able to cross the threshold at the next station.

There's a subcategory of passenger who, either to pass the time or because he's a genuine sexual pervert, tries to take advantage of the close proximity and to crowd his female victims, in the hope that, impressed by the size or hardness of his organ, they will be persuaded to agree to a rendezvous with him or, completely overcome, will even interrupt their journey and alight with the persuasive traveler before reaching their destination. To this subcategory seemed to belong the tall, brown-haired man who, drawn as if by a magnet, was attempting to position himself behind Ana. She'd gotten into the carriage at the previous station. She quickly realized that she had no chance of obtaining a seat, and so she opted for the simplest strategy: she remained standing by the doors. When the train stopped at the next station, the tall man, who—now it became visible!—had a birthmark on the left side of his forehead, finally managed to position himself behind her and observed that her bottom, protuberant and swathed in a very sheer material, was indeed highly suited to the maneuver he wished to make. Unfortunately, however, the doors opened and people shoved their way aboard, coming between her and the tall man. Peeved, the man was obliged to make further exhausting efforts in order to reposition himself behind Ana. He pressed himself up against her. His powerful erection awakened the curiosity of the beautiful blond, who, in a trice, reached behind her and grasped the member. The tall man gasped. With pleasure, obviously. But also in amazement. He bent his head and before the train came to a stop once more, he whispered something in her ear. She laughed, giving a perky shake of her head.

Ana's mother wasn't of noble stock . . .

—What does it matter? said Yegor, half asleep.

He was yawning fit to dislocate his jaw. Then he changed position, propping himself up on one elbow.

Furthermore, Ana's father had met her mother in rather mysterious circumstances, which neither he nor she saw fit to recount to their daughter. What's for sure is that she had a different surname . . . Obviously, that's only natural, but she also had a different first name.

Then how did Ana know?

A cousin on her father's side, an old maid, soured by age

and the insipid life she'd led, had told her a few things, when she made an unannounced visit one day and Ana's mother had to go out: she had a dental appointment and couldn't stay. Ana had been left alone with Aunt Tita. She was twelve or thirteen at the time, no older. Aunt Tita, who liked to gossip, told her everything under the sun. The girl listened, said nothing, asked no questions, showed no surprise, and didn't try to understand more than she understood. That evening, however, she'd been tempted to ask her mother whether the stories Aunt Tita had told her were true, but either she didn't find the right moment or she didn't dare; it wasn't very easy for her. She didn't ask her that evening, or the next day, or the day after. In the end, what her aunt told her slipped her mind. It isn't that she forgot it, but she simply didn't think about it anymore.

Did Jean-Jacques catch Yegor in Ana's arms? In a dream, naturally. Or to be more precise, he witnessed their amorous embrace, which began tenderly and gradually turned into a violent scuffle: the woman's legs are now perched on the man's shoulders, and he's shoving her like a wheelbarrow, plunging into her with a force and brutality to which she too contributes, slave to the dominant male, since her hands, hooked into his buttocks like claws, are dragging him toward her, inside her, still insatiable, desirous of even greater violence. Greater and greater . . . They're not groans of pleasure, gasps of voluptuousness, but cries of pain, of fear, at least this is how Jean-Jacques interprets them, and he's about to rush toward the two, who have reached the highest, paroxysmal point of coitus.

—Kill me! Kill me! moans the woman and Jean-Jacques awakes, sweating, terrified.

It isn't out of the question that Ana might have been a doctor but never practiced her profession. This, more or less, is what may be concluded from another post-coital conversation, which occurred somewhat later. Ana and Yegor were lying there . . . In bed, obviously, where else?

It's true that at her parents' insistence she sat the entrance examination, having crammed like crazy, and even succeeded in entering Bucharest's medical school, places at which were highly sought after in the 1970s. Unfortunately, in her second year, something terrible happened to her (I won't tell the story just yet!) and she began to miss lectures. It was a harsh winter, with blizzards and a lot of snow, in places the snowdrifts were higher than people's windows and they were unable to leave their houses. The people on the ground floor were forced to dig tunnels to get out, while the people on the first floor stepped outside through their windows into the snow.

—I'm exaggerating, but not much . . .

It had become impossible for traffic to circulate. Some of Bucharest's inhabitants got around on skis. Not that many people went to work or college, when it didn't stop snowing for days in a row. A deluge of snow! But she didn't show up for the winter term exams, which were held almost a month later, in February, when the snow had almost completely melted. When spring arrived at last and then summer, she didn't show up for the next round of exams. Nor did she attempt to pass the exams in autumn. She gave up. At home they had no idea that she'd abandoned her studies. Her mother knew about what had happened to her in late autumn, but no more than that. She didn't know about all the consequences of that misfortune. She knew only that she hadn't attended the winter term. She herself had told her daughter to stay at home. If she'd known she had no intention of attending later, maybe she'd have tried to persuade her to resume courses, after an interruption of more than two months, for which she had a bona fide medical certificate: she'd been admitted to hospital with severe depression. When she left hospital, her parents thought she was going to resume her course and was determined to prepare for her exams. She let them think that. She didn't tell them anything. And they didn't nag her; they didn't question her. It wasn't their style . . .

After two years of drifting she decided to take a nursing course. She enrolled, took the exams, and it was only later, toward the end of the course, that she told her parents that she was about to finish nursing school rather than a medical degree . . .

—That's the truth, she said, propping herself on one elbow and looking Yegor straight in the eye. He faced down her stare, her eyes as deeply blue as the Black Sea at Odessa.

—You might have said so from the start. There's hardly any shame in it. Nursing is a highly respectable job.

She closed her eyes, penitently.

—Do you have your nursing certificate here?

—No, I forgot to take it with me when I left Romania.

—How could you leave your certificate behind in Romania! You were determined to remain here in the West. It's like going hunting without a gun . . .

—I said I forgot to take it, didn't you hear?

—In the end, it's not all that serious . . . You can go back and get it. Romania is only two hours, in fact no, three hours away by plane.

Ana shrugged. Yegor got out of bed and took a few steps toward the window, turned around, leaned against the door of the closet, and crossed his arms across his chest. Her nonchalance was really beginning to drive him insane. He no longer knew what to believe, especially since not even now was he certain that Ana was telling the truth: had she really attended nursing college? Did she really have a certificate? Or was she lying now too? The doubts passed through his mind, but he didn't voice them. And why did she pretend to read books in German? Or wasn't she pretending? In which case maybe she spoke German and had been lying when she said that she hadn't stayed in Germany because she didn't know the language . . . Why in fact hadn't she stayed there? She knew enough German to be able to read it . . . But she couldn't converse in the language. That didn't hold much water . . . If you can read a novel in German, then you can string a few sentences together if need be. In any case, it still would have been better for her to remain in Frankfurt. If Jean-Jacques hadn't been mistaken and she really had been reading in German in the café. What novel had she been reading? She shrugged as if she'd been asked some outlandish question that didn't warrant the effort of an answer.

He still didn't ask her the direct question. His tongue was itching to say it, but still he didn't dare. Not even now, after she'd confessed that she wasn't a doctor. That she was neither a doctor nor a nurse. Because she wasn't a nurse if she'd left her certificate behind in Romania. If she couldn't prove her qualification . . . He didn't have the courage because it seemed to him that the question was too brutal. And it was brutal, because in his mind it was accompanied by all kinds of doubts, each more insulting than the next. He asked her the question in all its brutality, but only in his mind. And the answers were unbearable, primarily to him. That was why he didn't dare to ask her, curtly and straightforwardly: Then what do you do for a living? From the silver fox-fur coat to the rent on that desirably located apartment, everything seemed to point to a life, if not of luxury, then in any case one devoid of any material deprivation. Of course, she may not have bought the fur coat there, during the winter that had just ended; she may very well have brought it with her from Romania, it might have been her mother's. But what about the rent? Who paid the rent?

—Don't you have anybody in Romania who could send you that wretched certificate as soon as possible?

He'd asked the question to gain time and also to keep up the pressure. He was, you might say, circling the target, nurturing the absurd hope that Ana might give him the answer before he asked the question.

She didn't even tell Yegor that she'd been assaulted in an RER. What had she been doing on the train to Roissy at that hour of night? her increasingly jealous Russian lover would have asked. She didn't tell Yegor, but she went to the police station to file a complaint.

—There were three of them. Only one of them was really black. They snatched my handbag, in which there wasn't anything of great value. Money, I mean. They rummaged through it and found out that I live in the sixteenth arrondissement. "Filthy Yid!" they shouted at me. Two of them held me while the third drew three swastikas on me . . . On my chest and my belly . . .

—On your chest?

—Yes, you can't see it now, because I washed it off. I wasn't going to go around with that disgusting thing on my chest for all the world to see! One of them even wanted to draw a hammer . . .

—A what? said the policeman busy typing up her statement on the computer.

—A hammer and sickle . . . "She's from Romania," he said. "She's a communist Yid!"

—That's what he said?

—Exactly that!

The policeman's hands were moving with great speed and agility over the computer keyboard. From time to time his eyes gleamed with admiration.

—And are you . . . Jewish?

—I'm not Jewish. I'm from Romania. There aren't any Jews left there. Not even half-Jews! Just a few thousand old people, too elderly to leave the country. And too poor . . . The only place where they could go would be Israel. That's the truth . . . They had knives too. Maybe even pistols . . . bombs . . .

—Who?

—The Arabs.

—They were Arabs? asked the policeman, and again looked at her greedily.

—Arabs or whatever they were. Why do you want to know?

She had a rather large mole hidden beneath her right breast. When she was standing, the mole wasn't visible: it was covered by the breast, which, being quite voluminous, hung over it, covering or merely shading it. It was only really visible when she lay on her back. Jean-Jacques was sniffing her nipples, as if they were flowers. And her armpits. He ran his tongue over one of the nipples, sucked it, nibbled it. He then moved down toward the mole, which he didn't touch; the tongue, that red slug, came to a stop just before it. It went around the mole. Ana didn't so much as flinch. She looked like a cadaver who had just been pulled out on one of those drawers at the morgue. Jean-Jacques pulled her body out of that long box, which nonetheless didn't resemble a coffin, and carried her to the bed. No, she didn't smell of death. That was for sure . . . She smelled of flowers. What kind of flowers? He didn't know what they were called exactly. Maybe violets . . . Exactly, she smelled of violets. The woman wasn't moving. Her immobility excited him in the extreme. But he controlled himself. He was groaning. He stretched out next to the woman, who was as motionless as a corpse, and for a long time he lay stock-still. It was snowing slowly, extremely slowly . . .

Yegor hadn't yet appeared in the dream. But it wouldn't be long before he did . . . Here he was! He turned his head and saw him in the darkest corner of the room: he was squatting, resting his head on his hands, lost in thought. Or maybe he was in fact spying on him. It was his turn.

She hadn't even told Johannes that she'd been a medical student; the idea came to her later, after she arrived in Paris. She wanted to show off in front of Yegor, to bring him down a notch. She didn't really succeed . . . On the other hand, she did tell Johannes about the rape in the hunchback's house, but without telling him that the rapist applied for a visa to go to Israel a few years later. She told him only that his parents had come from Bessarabia at the same time as the Soviet tanks, in forty-four, when the Germans were scattering like partridges.

—That means he was Russian! exclaimed the German in satisfaction.

—I don't know what he was . . . He was horrible, that's what he was! He invited us to his house, ostensibly to dance. He had a big house and his parents were away; they had a villa near Bucharest. They were bigwigs. Nomenklatura . . .

Moved, Johannes caressed her hair, then her shoulders, he touched her skin with the palm of his hand and held his nose close, because he liked how she smelled: of acacia honey.

In a parking lot that reeked quite strongly of petrol, two women were talking. Or rather, they looked as if they were each waiting for somebody who was late and had thus taken the occasion to get to know each other. One of them, the older of the two, took a pack of cigarettes out of her handbag, then changed her mind and put it back.

—What did you say your name was?

—Ana.

—Mine's Catherine. I wasn't expecting you to be so well built . . . The small ad didn't exaggerate . . .

—You're not so bad yourself . . .

—You don't have to compliment me. Better you tell me whether you've brought any condoms with you.

—I've got a few.

—They're essential! Don't be stupid enough to . . . Don't let them talk you into . . . Understand? You don't mess around when it comes to that disease!

—I know.

—It's a terrible disease, take my word for it . . .

—I know, I know!

Catherine bent over Ana's cleavage, but not to admire her

breasts, which were rather on the large side for her taste, but to look more closely at the spot where they divided, above the sternum.

—What's that?

—What does it look like? A swastika. I drew it with a felt-tip pen.

—Why?

—I was just playing . . .

—You're playing with fire, said Catherine pensively.

Ana shrugged and took two or three paces to the right and then a few paces to the left. She looked a little nervous, in any case more nervous than she'd been up to then.

—Look, they're coming. The two cars: see them?

—Yes.

—It's them! A pity Wolfgang isn't with them . . .

—How do you know he's not?

—He'd have told me.

—Never mind. He'll come another time.

—What else is there then? she asked.

—Why should there be anything else?

Dieter said nothing more for a few minutes. His despairing, atheist speech, an apocalyptic speech probably intended to impress her, the woman from the East, had backfired on him in the end: it was blatantly obvious that he couldn't be bothered with anything anymore. He got up to make some coffee. It took a number of attempts before he managed to light the gas, which spurted, whistled, and finally ignited with such a big flame that it licked his eyebrows and forehead. He was lucky it didn't set his hair alight.

—God has punished you!

—Bollocks!

—You'll catch fire one of these days.

One Monday, coming home early, Ana caught the cleaning woman, Edith, holding the tape recorder to her ear, listening. Listening? Good for her! What could she hear? Just at that moment, the panting and groaning of a man making love came from the device. At intervals, more or less in counterpoint, a woman let out little shrieks, but whether they were of excitement, pleasure, or pain would have been hard to say.

—What are you doing? said Ana in indignation, but Edith was unfazed, since she didn't reckon it was any big deal, and in any case, it wasn't anything forbidden to listen to a tape left in full view on the bedside table.

—It's amusing, she said in the most natural tone in the world. I'm going to buy one myself. It can't be very expensive. Although I've never seen one so small. Except in the movies. Yes, in James Bond movies. Maybe you can't even find them in the shops.

She stopped chattering and looked at Ana, who didn't deign to talk about it. She simply turned on her heel. But she didn't leave the room. Edith shrugged.

The eagle's cage was on the windowsill. The bird had spread its wings, without yet managing to fill the whole space of its prison, which was getting smaller and smaller for it with each passing day. Through the window it saw the blue sky, the sparrows and other small avian creatures that were having fun, they were free, they gambolled, they flew where they wanted, without hindrance.

—He's not going to have any room, he's grown, murmured Ana.

Edith didn't understand what she was talking about straightaway. Not that she was really paying attention. She was reluctant to let go of that box, from which were now issuing words in an unfamiliar language. Italian? No, it wasn't Italian . . . Edith gave a rather stupid smile. On the tape, a man was chortling. Ana reached out her hand and took possession of the device, which she immediately turned off and thrust inside her handbag.

—I'll be finished soon, said Edith. I just have to do the vacuuming.

Ana went into the room with the small but well-stocked bookcase. She took a book from a shelf and started to read it. Or rather she flicked through it, because she was turning the pages too quickly to read them; probably she was looking for a certain page or paragraph. Or maybe a slip of paper between the pages. Or a letter. She didn't find anything. From the other room came the sound of the vacuum cleaner. She took the tape recorder out of her handbag. She was furious. With herself: how could she be so careless as to leave it lying around the place? She pressed a button. The voice was harsh and mocking at the same time. The laughter merely emphasized the mockery in the words. It was the voice of Mihai; it was lucky he was speaking Romanian.

Whenever Yegor announced he'd be coming around, Ana put the birdcage with the eagle in the closet. Rather an unpleasant operation, since the birdcage was heavy, and the closet was full of things. There was all kinds of junk that ought to have been thrown away, magazines, books that didn't have any room in the bookcase and were unworthy of being on display, things that no longer had any use, a couple of ashtrays, a vase, a broken hairdryer, a heap of coat hangers, suitcases piled on top of each other, and a chair. Ana placed the birdcage on the chair. The eagle looked at her somewhat reproachfully, shook its feathers, puffed them up, and then resigned itself, huddling limply, like a hen. The birdcage was still big enough for it, and it was far from being a condor. It looked more like a hawk or a kite than a genuine eagle, which, with its wings outspread, wouldn't even have had room in that barred space. Maybe it was a young eagle, which hadn't yet grown. In which case the situation was even more complicated. What would she do with it when it grew? This was a common-sense question that she didn't ask herself and I don't think she'd have troubled her head to find an answer, unless somebody else had asked her, Yegor for example. But Yegor was completely unaware of the eagle's existence.

It was a day in late spring, the first days of June, and it had already grown warm. Yegor regretted having put on his knitted tank top, which made him feel hot, unbearably hot. He stopped. He dismounted next to a blond, who was taller than him, and who thought that he'd stopped for her. She murmured enticements and stated a figure, which, evidently, stood for a sum of money. Yegor paid no attention to her. The woman got annoyed, turned around, and walked away a few paces. Yegor's head was no longer visible, being completely covered by the tight tank top, within which it was now stuck. The woman turned back around to ask him what he was up to, why he was there. She seemed irritated, but when she saw him with his head stuck inside the tank top, she burst out laughing. The man's tousled head appeared once more. He didn't know what to do with that wretched jersey.

—Hot, aren't you? said the woman, with concern. She can't have been more than eighteen or nineteen. She was wearing a raincoat, and underneath it a pair of shorts: long legs and big tits, crammed inside a small bra.

—Yes, I'm hot, admitted Yegor and looked at the girl more closely. She wasn't his type: too tall, too thin. Nothing but tits . . .

—Looking for anyone in particular?

He didn't answer. He mounted his bicycle and rode away, pedaling harder and harder. He almost crashed into another cyclist, who barely managed to swerve in time. And he continued to pedal with a fury, as if he were in a race against invisible opponents.

What can have got into her to ask whether he was Jewish! Yegor looked at her in astonishment. He hadn't been expecting such a question. And he couldn't understand what she was getting at.

They were both naked. Yegor wasn't embarrassed in the slightest to show himself naked in front of her, even during moments when they were not amorously engaged. In fact, neither of them hid from the other's gaze. You might say they were quite satisfied with how they looked.

—Me? Why would I be Jewish? I'm not . . .

—It's nothing to be embarrassed about!

—I didn't say it was . . .

—You didn't say it, but you act all indignant and defensive as if I'd accused you of something infamous.

—But what if I'm not Jewish! Don't you understand? Look . . . look at it more closely, if you haven't had a spare moment to examine it before now.

And Yegor lifted up his member, whose glans, although in repose, was unsheathed. But the foreskin was intact. It was evident that he hadn't been circumcised. Was it so evident? To a specialist it would've been . . . Ana took it in her hand to get a better look. She moved her forehead closer, her eyes, her lips.

—It's quite pretty! she said admiringly and held the glans between her lips. At the same time she tried to say something.

—Don't talk with your mouth full!

Naturally, Ana didn't have any comeback to that, but there was no point in her getting annoyed; it was his usual jesting. But when she regained her power of speech she did seem a little annoyed. Perhaps because that rather bizarre discussion wasn't yet done with. She for one would have had a few more things to say on the subject now that it had come up.

—There are also Jews who aren't circumcised, she said with the utmost conviction. I've known a number of men in that situation, she added, at the same time caressing his member, which, to all appearances, was what the man lying beside her liked best of all. But, I think it's possible to say that even so . . .

—Where? in Romania?

—Yes, in Romania. After the persecution during the war . . .

—Persecution you call it . . .

Yegor appeared to want to take his revenge. Ana immediately corrected herself:

—After the horrors during the war, there were Jewish parents who refused to circumcise male babies.

—And you think that this applies to me?

—I don't know . . .

—You don't know, but you say it anyway. You say whatever comes into your head. You don't bother to think even for one second. I wasn't born in Romania. I was born in Russia, in the U.S.S.R., if you prefer. And anyway, in Romania the Jews were exterminated. Sent to the camps, gassed . . . There weren't many left for you to study . . .

—You're talking nonsense, said Ana, annoyed. You're getting Romania mixed up with Germany, with Poland. I don't know what goes on in that head of yours.

She seemed very annoyed, and so Yegor didn't dwell on it. But Ana was probably in the mood to talk, and the subject seemed to fascinate her.

—Circumcision is also demanded by the Koran, she added.

—That's true . . .

—You see? Tell me, then: how do you recognize a Jew?

—Why do you have to recognize somebody is a Jew?

—You don't have to . . . But it means my question isn't wholly absurd. I asked you purely out of curiosity. You could've given me a simple answer, without getting upset or protesting as if I'd insulted you. Really, anybody would think you were a racist . . .

—A minute ago I was a Jew, and now you're calling me a racist . . .

—There are racist Jews too!

—Anyway, the Jews aren't a race. It's a religion!

—Really? What about atheists? Or aren't there any Jewish atheists?

—There's no talking to you . . .

—Why? Because I'm a woman?

—You Romanians are a frivolous people.

—Frivolous? Why frivolous? On the contrary, I'm trying to be as logical as possible . . .

—You're not logical, you're a sophist!

—Really? Like I said, you're a racist! Just the other day you called Romanians Gypsies. Now you see them as Gypsy sophists. I ask myself which is worse: to be a Gypsy or to be a sophist?

Utterly indignant, Ana got out of bed and started to get dressed. Looking for her panties, she set eyes on the tape recorder. She picked it up and calmly deposited it in the drawer of a small dressing table or cabinet, I'm not exactly sure what to call it. She looked out of the corner of her eye at Yegor, who was still in bed, contemplating his member.

That kind of blouse is called an *ie* and there was a time when it was more popular in Paris than in Romania; all right, let's not exaggerate: women don't wear them in Bucharest or in towns anymore, but in the country, in the villages of northern Moldavia and in Maramureș in particular, women still wear them from time to time, on Sundays or feast days, when they go to church. Or at traditional ring dances. At least so I've been told . . . When I went there, I had more to do with *horincă* drinkers. Sometimes, in the evenings, when we'd taken a skinful, we went to the village bar, where the women from Bessarabia performed striptease acts. There was no evidence of any traditional ring dances. The women wrapped themselves around a metal pole, contorted themselves in all kinds of ways. They had magnificent bodies . . . And not one inhibition! They came and sat in our laps, mounted us . . .

The woman with the *ie* is seated on a sofa, leaning somewhat to the side. Behind her can be seen a window. On the windowsill there's a birdcage. It's above the shoulder of the woman, whose features, as I've already said, are blurred, vague, barely discernable. Anyhow, nobody was looking at her, but rather at her blouse or at the birdcage. If it had been up to me, I'd have put an eagle rather than a parrot in the birdcage. But the birdcage was too small for an eagle, the painter must have thought. Even if it had been just an eagle or a hawk chick, it would still have needed a bigger cage. In which case, not only would there not have been enough room on the windowsill—ultimately, he could have opened the window before starting to paint—but also it wouldn't have been completely visible, since it would have been partly obscured by the woman wearing the *ie*. For there wasn't enough room for both. And then the painter wouldn't have been able to see the eagle, which, naturally, would have been moving around, it would hardly have sat motionless in just the visible part of the birdcage . . .

A tall man dressed with what we shall call English elegance entered the café. It was almost lunchtime. Ana was still sitting at her table. Reading. The elegant man walked over to her without hesitating. He came to a stop half a meter away. He coughed to attract her attention and finally she looked up. They looked at each other for a few seconds without saying a word. On her forehead you could now see the brown blotch, which was quite large: you couldn't help but think of the outline of Romania. With or without Bessarabia . . .

—So, in the end you kept your word . . .

—Yes.

—Did you have any difficulty finding the address?

The gentleman shrugged and asked whether he might take a seat. He sat down. He looked around for the barman, turning his head in every direction. Jean-Jacques wasn't at the bar. Ed emerged from the back of the café and went over to the table where the two were sitting. "How young he is!" thought Ana. "He's probably a student and works as a waiter to support himself while he's at college." Ed stood straight-backed, motionless, waiting to take the order. Perhaps he was looking at the blotch on the customer's forehead, although he gave the impression that his mind was somewhere else entirely.

—A coffee! said the elegant gentleman finally, more to please the young waiter than because he felt like drinking coffee.

Ed went to the bar, where Jean-Jacques had returned in the meantime and was watching the scene, his neck rigid with tension.

—A coffee, said Ed.

—Doesn't she want anything?

Ed didn't bother to answer. He waited for the coffee, leaning his elbows on the counter. Although he knew very well that once the percolator had filled the cup with that bitter liquid he detested (he'd still not been able to overcome his childhood aversion), the café proprietor would take it over to the table himself, he wouldn't let him do it. And that's what happened. Jean-Jacques took the cup of coffee to the table himself. In the midst of a conversation with the elegant gentleman, Ana didn't so much as glance at him. Jean-Jacques didn't dare address her, to say anything to her, for example, to ask whether she wanted anything else, be it only a glass of water. He went back to the bar. Around now Yegor would be making his appearance! Jean-Jacques rubbed his hands. He picked up a glass and filled it with tap water. Any moment now Yegor would enter the café and goggle in disbelief: the elegant gentleman had laid his long, delicate, bony hand on Ana's forearm and she made not the slightest gesture of protest. Jean-Jacques watched greedily. You would've thought that he couldn't react unless Yegor were there. By himself, he didn't deign to be jealous. Whereas with Yegor around, it was something else entirely . . . Would both of them have watched the two cooing doves? Hmm . . . Jean-Jacques would probably have stared at Yegor more than at them. It was a kind of revenge against Yegor. And he rubbed his hands again. At first sight, he seemed delighted. Rather stupid, but anyway . . . Rather puerile! Probably he himself realized it. He decided not to gawp at the two, although they didn't even care if anybody was looking at them. They were looking at each other, deep into each other's eyes, or at least so it appeared. Jean-Jacques dropped a glass in the sink. The noise didn't startle anybody, and certainly not them. A glass breaking in a bistro: what could be less unusual?

After a while, Jean-Jacques thought to glimpse Yegor through the window. Then the café door slowly opened, but nobody entered. The door closed again and Jean-Jacques didn't have time to see who it was. He craned his neck, but it was too late. He was about to rush to the door. But he changed his mind.

At the back of the café, Ed took from his pocket a notebook with a blue cover, a yellow ballpoint pen, and jotted something down. He had tiny handwriting: the letters were like tiny red ants scurrying across the page.

—Hasn't the Romanian woman come? asked one of the men, coming out of the showers with a towel over his left shoulder and his huge schlong swaying from side to side. He rubbed himself rather carelessly: drops of water gleamed on his body.

Where was La Belle Roumaine?

That's what all the men called her, and the women were rather jealous, and in any case quite peeved. When they said it, La Belle Roumaine sounded ironic, but not mocking.

He climbed the stairs, thinking about her in a fury. Spoiling for an argument. He rang the bell and had to wait almost two minutes before Ana deigned to open the door. He drummed on the door with his fingers, snorted, hammered on the solid wood with his fist. He even kicked the door once.

—Why don't you give me a key? he barked at her by way of a greeting.

Ana was wearing a bathrobe. She didn't bother to reply. In fact, two weeks previously, he'd voiced the same grievance and the same demand, and Ana had calmly answered that she wasn't the owner of the apartment. She had only the one key. For herself. And he'd accepted her answer or given her to believe that he accepted it. In reality, the argument didn't have a leg to stand on. She only had the one key? What was stopping her from making a copy? Maybe she wanted to insinuate that she didn't trust him . . . That she didn't want him coming around when she wasn't at home. That she didn't want him rummaging through her drawers, looking through her personal effects, finding some compromising document or other. But did she have anything to hide? He didn't ask her that question immediately. When he did ask it, a few days later, she shrugged, turned her back, went into the bathroom. With dignity.

I might insert myself into the game at this point . . . After all, I know quite a few more things than poor Yegor. I'd be able to ask her questions she'd find it much harder to answer. With regard to the eagle? Not necessarily. No, I don't think she was afraid that he'd enter the closet and find the eagle. Because she'd locked it and put the key in a case which she kept in a safe place. And anyway, what if he did come across the eagle? Isn't she allowed to keep a bird in the house? Some people keep a parrot. Others even a crow . . . Once, out of the blue, Yegor had tried the handle of the closet, was surprised to find it locked, but she was in bed at that moment, enticing, alluring . . . She was slowly moving her thighs, rubbing one against the other. Yegor soon forgot about the closet.

But one day she forgot to lock the door, and he leaned on the handle for some reason, the door had opened and Yegor almost fell through to the other side, which was in darkness. He felt the wall for the light switch but couldn't find it . . .

—What are you doing in there? she yelled.

—Nothing, he replied, abashed.

He hadn't done it deliberately. Let's not imagine that he was burning with a desire to go inside the closet. Ultimately, he wasn't even curious by nature. Why would he root around in that wretched closet? What was he supposed to find? Another lover in his long johns? A half-decayed corpse? Maybe hidden treasure . . .

He went up to her and to mollify her he started to caress her. She was still quivering with annoyance. But after a few minutes they held each other in their arms, they clenched each other in a passionate embrace, each knowing all the little tricks that would amplify and prolong their pleasure. They were, both the one and the other, professionals of amour, a field in which neither had anything left to learn.

The first thing that caught Yegor's eye was the copy of *Paris-Turf*. The man was walking slowly, tottering slightly, as if sloshed. He was walking along the path from the direction of Auteuil. He'd left the track before the penultimate race. He no longer had any money to lay a bet. He'd lost everything, down to the last penny. He hesitated for a moment, and then Yegor saw him fling his rolled-up newspaper on the grass. In a fury. He walked for another few paces and then stopped, went back, and stooped to pick up the newspaper. It was at this point that Yegor passed him. He turned his head to look at the other side of the road, where he'd espied from the corner of his eye two or three floozies, rather nicely stacked ones, wearing trench coats and silk or waterproof raincoats with not much else underneath. The three graces kept a certain distance apart from each other. They didn't talk to each other; they didn't look at each other. From time to time they opened their trench coats, as if they were hot, and gave a flash of thigh and belly button. Yegor decided it was time to cross the road. The racing man had receded into the distance, absorbed in his newspaper. In that instant, a car pulled up, a "belle américaine," and one of the three nimbly climbed inside, slamming the door behind her. The car drove off with a screech of tires. Suddenly Yegor realized that the woman had looked like Ana . . . Or maybe it really was she! He went up to one of the women left behind on the pavement. What he was doing was pointless; it was stupid. Completely stupid!

—How should I know what she's called? snapped the woman.

—Please forgive me, but I thought you knew each other.

Whores like you to be polite with them. However, it wasn't Yegor's politeness that touched the girl, but rather his diffidence, the awkward way in which he was trying to question her. One thing was for sure: he wasn't with the police.

—Come with me if you want me to forgive you. You won't regret it, I guarantee!

Yegor moved away without another word. He'd come back. He knew a café nearby; he'd go there and drink a coffee. After which he'd go back.

—I'll be back, he called, and the woman jabbed the side of her head with her forefinger. I'll be back, don't worry!

"He's got a screw loose!" the woman said to herself.

But Yegor really did come back. About half an hour later. He asked the questions he wanted to ask about the woman who had climbed into the car not long since, and his interlocutor, stimulated by a crisp, gleaming banknote, answered without hesitation.

—Now come with me! the woman cajoled.

Yegor made no reply. He seemed very weary all of a sudden.

It was Edith who found her, one Monday. She was naked, in the bathtub, which was full of water that had turned red from the blood. One arm was hanging over the side of the tub and the dripping blood had formed a small puddle on the floor. Edith didn't scream. She merely raised her hand to her mouth. She didn't scream; she said: "Mon Dieu, mon Dieu." After a moment's hesitation, she approached the bathtub: on her forehead, near the temple, Ana had a huge bruise. It seemed to her that she was still breathing. She wasted no time: she rushed to the telephone and called the police. The policeman at the other end of the line was probably wary of hoax calls and asked her for the number she was telephoning from. Fortunately, Edith knew it by heart, she didn't hesitate. This reassured the policeman. He took down the address.

Edith sat on the armchair in the small living room. Next to her—she just had to stretch out her hand!—was Ana's handbag. She pulled it toward her, opened it, looked inside, just for something to do, so that she wouldn't have to think about the dead woman in the bathroom. All she found was a makeup kit. She looked more carefully. She found neither a purse nor the small tape recorder. There wasn't even an address book or a notebook, no matter how small. She then got up and looked around the apartment. What was she looking for? She wasn't looking for anything in particular. In any case, the tape recorder was nowhere to be found. She even looked under the bed. She pulled a few books out of the small bookcase and looked behind them. Then she put them back. She opened the door to the closet. She didn't see the birdcage with the eagle. It was rather strange, but she decided it was better that way . . . To hell with the eagle! But she felt sorry about the tape recorder. She liked it, it was amusing . . . She gave a wail. Time was wasting!

She didn't have time to make a thorough search. The police arrived quite quickly. They brought with them a stretcher and everything they needed in order to provide first aid. They lifted Ana out of the bloody bathtub and laid her on the stretcher. They fitted her with an oxygen mask and applied tourniquets to her arms. The cuts didn't look very deep, but the policemen were doing their duty. Then one of the policemen saw the bruise on the side of her head.

—This isn't a suicide, he said.

Edith was trembling in a corner.

II

SHE KNEW SHE'D FIND him at home, seated at his desk, which was heaped with books, notebooks, and bunches of pens and pencils of every color, inserted into ceramic mugs of the kind from which his compatriots rather drank beer, as was only normal, in any case they'd never use them as holders for obsessively sharpened pencils for underlining and annotating books, a habit she despised . . . He wasn't content only to scribble in the books he read, he also had to make notes, with a pen, rather than a pencil; he'd filled up a whole stack of notebooks with that small, tidy handwriting of his. She had no idea what he wrote down in them! In the two or three months she'd been living with him, she'd never looked in his notebooks, although he left them on his desk, sometimes with the pages open and on view. Out of respect? Out of discretion? No, she simply wasn't interested. Likewise, for a long time she didn't open any of the books in the two bookcases that were almost as large as the walls of the living room. Most of them were complicated philosophical books, with a vocabulary made up of words as long as a Romanian meat line, words which, even when she could half decipher them, she could still not understand or—even worse!—understood in completely the opposite way. Anyway, with her pidgin German, there was little chance of her understanding any of it . . .

—Germans don't understand it either, Johannes consoled her.

—Rubbish! You're just saying it . . .

—What I mean is Germans who lack a thorough philosophical grounding.

—They're still German words!

—Unlike Kant, explained Johannes, Hegel began to use German to denote or create the philosophical concepts he required . . . He was one of the first to open the way to the Germanization of concepts. Others came after him . . . But paradoxically, this Germanization, rather than facilitating understanding, led to the creation of a real jargon, which, without prior training, you either won't be able to understand or you will misinterpret in places.

—All very well, but didn't Kant write in German?

Johannes would give a benevolent chuckle, take her hand to kiss it or hasten to kiss her on the forehead, paternally or at least platonically. Hannah allowed herself to be humored and, of course, exaggerated her naivety, her candor, she saw very well that the Kraut liked it . . . Why not indulge him? She tried to please him in every possible way, both in the kitchen and in the sheets, and he too was grateful, he forced himself to overlook other less agreeable things, he pretended not to notice them, he kept his nose in his books and sometimes even managed to forget. But if you think about it, her question was natural; childish, but natural. You only have to take Descartes, who started out writing Latin. Leibniz never abandoned the classical tongue, and when he didn't write in Latin, he wrote in French rather than German . . . Her exaggerating her naivety or rather ignorance didn't prevent her from looking up all those great philosophers in the encyclopedia. And so in the end she did learn a few things. It was superficial knowledge, obviously, but better than not knowing anything . . . And as for him, instead of chuckling tenderly at her ignorance, he'd have done better to explain to her how philosophical terminology had evolved from the Middle Ages to Kant and then Hegel. How first Latin was abandoned and then even the so-called scholastic terms, which also came from Latin. It wouldn't have been any skin off his teeth!

Obviously, she didn't tell Johannes anything about her research into the history of philosophy . . . Not that it had lasted very long! Philosophy wasn't something that fascinated her. True, she didn't understand a great deal about it, she ought to have taken it progressively, starting with elementary notions. When she was at lyceum in Romania, philosophy wasn't a subject on the syllabus. Not even if you studied philosophy at university did you learn anything much apart from Marxism. The classic philosophers, who had played no other rôle than to help human thought and the human species to produce Marx, were studied solely through the writings of the latter. As if through a filter . . . Depending on the extent to which they'd approached the supreme truth of Marxism! Other philosophers reached the student only after being transcribed in a Marxist key and sometimes even censored: during courses, but above all in the textbooks. There's no point in even mentioning philosophers after Marx! They were all in error, sinners sent straight to hell.

What could poor Hannah do? She'd have needed patience if she were to set about studying it now, taking it from the elementary notions without which it's impossible to understand anything much of what comes after. A lot of patience . . . And how was she supposed to have patience if she wasn't interested in it! She didn't tell him about her searches through the bookcase, but Johannes knew about them nonetheless. Being a maniac when it came to tidiness and having an exceptional memory, he straightaway noticed that the encyclopedias were not in their proper places: they were in the wrong order on the shelf. Somebody had been tampering with them . . . And there were only the two of them in the house! Dieter came around occasionally, but even if he sometimes remained alone in the living room, Johannes couldn't imagine him rushing to the bookcase to consult the encyclopedias while he went to the toilet or another room. He'd have done so while Johannes was present . . . And anyway, he had his own encyclopedias at home, most of which were the same. He therefore had no doubt that Hannah had been leafing through the encyclopedias, which touched him even more tenderly, since on her part it demonstrated not only an interest in philosophy, but also an interest in him, in Johannes, the philosophy teacher, who had picked her up one day, or rather one evening, at the cinema . . .

Sitting at his desk, in his slippers and dressing gown, he'd been waiting for her for three days and three nights.

He had also used to wait for his mother, who often went missing from home, sometimes even at night. His father had died in an airplane accident in the United States while away on a business trip. Johannes had been no more than eight or nine at the time. And so you might say he was accustomed to waiting. He'd even written an essay on the subject of waiting. A rather Heideggerian essay, although he'd made an effort to avoid the terms that are part and parcel of the great philosopher's jargon. Waiting is specifically human and directly connected with the idea of death. Granted, when summed up like that, Johannes's essay loses its nuance and a great part of its subtlety. He'd published it in quite an obscure review, published in Freiburg at irregular intervals. Dieter had made fun of him about it, but perhaps he was a little jealous, so thought Johannes. His friend, a philosophy teacher like him, claimed that philosophy was finished and there was no point in beating your brains writing just to say what had already been said.

Hannah had gone missing at night only once before. She'd been with a girlfriend whose mother had died of cancer. Not at the hospital, but at home. Her friend had telephoned to tell her that she was scared to sleep alone. Other friends had gone to sleep over at her house too; they'd taken it in turns. Hannah went when it was her turn, when her friend called her. Maybe she was at Sarah's this time too . . . But why didn't she telephone? In fact, she'd telephoned the day before, but she hadn't said anything about Sarah, she'd been quite ambiguous, saying something about being invited to see a film about Europe, it was all too vague to understand. And that annoyed him.

—You're talking at sixes and sevens, he said rather curtly, but also emotionally, moving the receiver from one ear to the other and back again.

—What do you mean? What are you trying to say? I don't know that expression.

—I mean you're talking nonsense; it's impossible to understand what you're saying.

—I talk the best I can, she retorted, almost bursting into tears.

Johannes knew that Hannah was a very sensitive woman. A very emotive woman. You only had to raise your voice when talking to her and her eyes would fill with tears, a lump would form in her throat, preventing her from speaking, if she tried to say anything else, her words would get jumbled up, become all confused, her voice would gradually die away and it would be impossible to understand anything much. And so Johannes tried to mollify her.

—Yes, of course you do, it's just that I can't understand why . . .

—You can't understand? You can't understand because German isn't my mother tongue. It's the language of my mother's killers! declared Hannah and burst into tears.

Johannes fell silent. He'd have wished to tell her that it wasn't a question of language, it was just that he couldn't understand why she wasn't coming home, but he realized that he was on treacherous ground. Who knows what turn the conversation could have taken. He didn't have the courage to continue. He apologized, said it didn't matter if she didn't come home that night, it wasn't important, it was just that he was a little worried, but now that he'd heard her voice and knew that nothing was wrong . . .

Hannah hung up on him. That would teach him!

Johannes wasn't much older than she was; perhaps he wasn't older at all. It was hard to say how old that mysterious woman from the mouths of the Danube was . . . The charm in which she enveloped men was also due to a certain ambiguity. She cultivated or else was merely complicit in that indeterminacy regarding her origins. Johannes smiled, and then he bit his lip. He made an effort and refused to nitpick. What would have been the point? He sat back down at his desk. He removed his feet from his slippers.

Hannah had blue eyes and black hair, so black and so glossy that you would have thought she dyed it. Which doesn't mean that she'd have been blond or brunette otherwise. But anyway, her hair couldn't have been as black as ebony naturally. The contrast with her very white skin was delicious. She looked like a geisha. Or rather she looked like the geishas in erotic woodcuts . . . Johannes was impressed.

Hannah exerted over men a kind of fascination that our philosopher was unable to analyze. He didn't dare put it down to her Jewish origins. That kind of generalization was the door that led straight to racism. Otherwise, Hannah didn't have Semitic features. Then again, she was from the East, her ancestors had, at least a little, mingled with the Slavs, the Hungarians, the Romanians. Is racial purity non-existent or is it quite simply that race is non-existent? And anyhow, that charm of hers had nothing whatever to do with her physical features, with her beauty. Her charm was rather due to a certain girlishness on her part. Of course, he could see very well that she exaggerated her naivety, her candor, but that didn't mean much. Her exaggeration of her naivety was itself a form of naivety, a childish trait or something that had remained with her since childhood, when she'd observed that adults like children's naivety. A childish cunning . . . Instead of suspecting her of hypocrisy or being irritated at her pretending in order to please him, he feigned not to notice, he kept his nose in his philosophy books and sometimes he even managed not to observe any of the things that might otherwise have disturbed him. He knew how to look at her and pick out only the things that he liked. He managed not to see the rest. That derived from his strength of character, the same as his capacity to focus completely on what he was doing at a particular moment. He managed quickly to close all the parentheses in his mind, and so, no matter how much he liked the woman, it wouldn't be possible to say that she was an obsession for him. Or at least so he liked to believe . . .

He absorbed himself in his reading, conscientiously took notes, and from time to time paused to look out of the window. The sky was blue. He smiled, almost happy . . .

Dieter dropped in on his friend Johannes. As usual, it hadn't crossed his mind to telephone beforehand. They'd both been used to it since they were at lyceum. But ever since Hannah had moved into Johannes's house lock, stock, and barrel, such unannounced visits sometimes ran the risk of being embarrassing. Obviously, there was no risk that morning . . .

—Where's Hannah?

—Er . . . she's just gone out to do some shopping.

—I thought I saw her one evening in the lobby of a cinema. I was passing, in a hurry. She told me you were with her . . .

—I was with her?

—No. I don't know. I didn't see you.

Dieter didn't tell him that she'd been with another man when he saw her, a stranger, who looked like a Turk, he didn't tell him any of that.

—Well, I was . . . You didn't see me, but I was. I'd probably gone downstairs to the toilet. That's why you didn't see me.

—That's as may be, mumbled Dieter, rather embarrassed.

Johannes avoided his eyes. He stood up, went to the window, and then came back, shuffling his slippers, and said, as if apologizing:

—Hannah was dead set on seeing that film. She'd been nagging me about it for days. She was obsessed with it . . .

—What film?

—First of all, I told her: go and see it by yourself if you're so keen. Why do you need to drag me along? But she wasn't having any of it . . .

—And what film did you see?

—What film? Oh . . . a detective film. I can't remember what it was called. Hang on . . . *Hotel Europa*, or something of the sort . . . Yes, that's what it was called: *Hotel Europa.*

Then he blew a raspberry, as a token of his scornful opinion of the film. Dieter was feeling more and more awkward. He rummaged through his pockets and pulled out a rather rumpled packet of cigarettes. He looked at his friend from the corner of his eye and said:

—Anyway, it's not important.

—Quite a poor film, I must say . . . And pretentious to boot! That's what annoyed me the most. If it had been a little less pretentious, maybe it would've been acceptable. I'd have made an effort. But as it was . . . I almost fell asleep at one point. It's pointless your smiling! Films like that bore me. They're also tiring.

—Tiring?

—Yes, tiring, because you have to pay attention, to concentrate, not to let your mind stray, to remember all kinds of details, otherwise you won't know what's going on . . . All that effort to find out what? What do you find out in the end? Can you tell me?

—The solution to the riddle, sniggered Dieter. You find out who is the murderer . . .

—What do I care who is the murderer, who committed the crime! The author committed it! He's the murderer. At any rate, he's the moral perpetrator. He set things up in such a way as to allow the murder to take place. That's the naked truth . . .

Johannes was getting worked up, he was capable of perorating for days and nights on end about detective films, which he hated, the same as he hated American films in general, with or without special effects, anything produced in Hollywood . . .

But right then his friend wasn't in the mood for a discussion about detective films or American cinema. Especially since he thought that Johannes was lying about Hannah and the evening at the cinema. There was something not quite right about the whole business! He'd ponder it later, in detail, in order to work out what it was all about.

—Everything about detective films is artificial, the same as novels in the same genre. They're manufactured, made to a recipe . . .

—The art of pastry making . . .

—Not to mention the fact that all the films are alike, so much so that you're always watching one and the same film.

—You get to discover America, said Dieter, making fun of him, before adding that detective films were not a subject worthy of lengthy debate. We're wasting time! he concluded, and then stood up. He went to the small bar that occupied a space in the middle of the bookcase and poured himself a glass of whiskey.

After which they talked about something completely different.

She was missing from home for only three nights. On the third night, when he saw that she wasn't coming home, so as not to lie in bed looking up at the ceiling, Johannes had taken a double dose of sleeping pills, two pills at once. Before falling into a dreamless sleep, he remembered the telephone conversation with Hannah and tried to find the smallest clue that might allow him to discover some significant detail connected to her absence. He found none. He calmed himself by telling himself that Hannah had to be taken as she was: with all her qualities and small defects. At any rate, the qualities were more important. She was imaginative and unpredictable. Wasn't that what had attracted him to her? Then why was he complaining?

He recalled how Hannah, as if it had been the most natural thing in the world, had told him the story of how in Romania she'd been in an elevator that plummeted to a basement full of water, which had been flooded for days, since nobody had come to fix the pipes. That was what it was like in those days . . .

—Under Ceaușescu?

—Under Ceaușescu, who else!

The elevator had fallen and the water had cushioned the impact. She hadn't been hurt. But she'd gotten a fright and was left with a phobia toward elevators. If she could dispense with the elevator, she was highly satisfied. She preferred to climb the stairs . . .

—What floor did you fall from?

—The third floor. A mere bagatelle.

The water came up to her chin, and the firemen who came to rescue her found her like that, standing on tiptoes, with Missy on her head . . .

—Missy?

Missy, her favorite cat. When she climbed inside the elevator, she'd been cradling her in her arms, but now that the water came up to her neck, she couldn't hold her anymore.

—Understand?

The cat had sat still, on top of her head. From time to time she mewled, because she was afraid of water. She mewled and dipped her paw in the dirty, stinking water. But she hadn't been brave enough to swim through the water and clamber up the lift grille and out into the light.

—Go, Missy. Go! Save yourself at least . . .

Johannes had clutched his sides with laughter. He felt like laughing even now, just thinking about it. He sank into sleep with a smile on his lips.

Unfortunately, her stories were not always amusing and bizarre. When she told him about everything her parents had been through, Johannes wanted the earth to swallow him up, so ashamed was he. Strictly speaking, only her father had died in the gas chambers at Auschwitz, her mother's husband to be more precise. After his death, her mother never married again. She became pregnant with her later, after the age of thirty-five, with a Pole from Danzig, who was just passing through Romania. At least that's what her mother told her or gave her to understand, in order to avoid any discussion of it . . . When she was little, aged two or three, she used to talk to him in German, if you can call what a child says at such a tender age talking . . . Let's say he used to talk to her in German. She couldn't remember very well. She relied mostly on her mother's memories. In her own memory all that remained was the outline of a tall, a very tall, thin man. Her father . . . But her mother distorted that image without putting in its place another image closer to the reality.

Tall? He wasn't at all tall . . . "What reality, anyway!" her mother would say scornfully, raising her eyebrows and puckering her lips. Hannah would burst out laughing at how adamant she was. Not even she knew why her mother's rage against reality seemed so comical . . . Against what existed, in other words. Would she have rather nothing existed than what really existed? Johannes nodded, but didn't interrupt; he let her continue. He liked her parentheses.

Having reached adolescence, she plagued her mother with all kinds of questions. To tell the truth, she would have liked to talk about him, about her father, but she begged her in vain, she implored her, and her mother changed the subject.

—What was her name?

Her name was Esther, yes, that was her name, and although she was no longer young, she was still a success with men. Or in any event she showed a great deal of interest in members of the opposite sex, who visited the house and were constantly coming and going. Hannah used to mix them up; there were too many of them. Esther refused to say more than two or three mostly meaningless words about Hannah's father, her real father:

—Why did he leave? the girl would ask.

—Leave where?

—Romania . . .

—Why don't you ask me why he left Poland?

—Why did he?

But her mother would refuse to talk about it any more.

"This pointless discussion," as she called it, and she'd get up from her armchair and leave the room.

—Was he German? asked Johannes, giving voice to the question that had been on the tip of his tongue.

—I don't know . . . What does it mean to be a German from Danzig?

—Lots of Germans lived in Danzig . . .

—Good for them!

Johannes then realized that he was in danger of stumbling into a minefield and that it would be more prudent not to dwell on the matter. Nonetheless he did ask whether her mother spoke German.

—She spoke German, of course she did. But we'd gotten used to speaking Romanian. Even when it was just the two of us. She didn't have any desire to learn that language which she'd ended up hating. That's the truth! Whatever I knew, I'd learned from Father, who spoke bad Romanian . . .

What's for sure is that not much remained of the German she'd learned back then, the "kitchen" German spoken by Richard or, more seldom, her mother.

—Richard? Oh, the German from Danzig!

—I didn't say he was German. Do you think Mother would've been able to put up with him if he'd been German? Go on, tell me, is that what you think?

Johannes wasn't brave enough to contradict her. If he'd been brave enough, he'd have said that in those years, in the Stalinist period, a Polish Jew wouldn't have had anything to fear. On the contrary, at least in the beginning, the regime would have catered to his every whim. And so he wouldn't have left Poland, where he had victim status and therefore advantages. Where would he have gone, anyway? To Romania? Whereas after the war the Germans were not viewed kindly by the Poles, all the more so if they lived in Gdansk, that is, in Danzig . . . The Germans had more reasons to leave than the Jews, to abandon Poland and try to reach West Germany. Anyhow, it's complicated: some Jews, especially if they weren't communists, wanted to leave then too, in the 1950s, I mean. It wasn't easy for many of them to bear living in the place where they'd trembled in fear of death for so long and where their families had been decimated. And so they left, they went wherever they could . . . They packed up and left!

If he'd been brave enough, Johannes would have said that he was German and she managed to put up with him . . . But he wasn't, and so he limited himself to murmuring:

—Richard had probably lived in hiding during the war. So as to escape with his life . . .

—In hiding? Where?

—I don't know, with some peasants, for example. Not all the Polish peasants handed over the Jews that sought shelter with them.

Hannah shrugged.

Johannes got up from his armchair and pretended he needed to go to the bathroom. It was more prudent that way . . . He'd gotten into a discussion that might deteriorate at any moment. It was better to interrupt it and even do everything possible not to resume it. Why should he bandage his head if it didn't hurt? Yes, yes, you might say, without overstating it, that Johannes lived in constant fear when it came to Hannah. Dieter upbraided him for it on numerous occasions . . . Granted, his friend was rather special; he often came out with all kinds of mischievous remarks, some of them downright dangerous.

—Dangerous?

And Dieter would laugh his head off.

One thing was for sure: Richard had quickly vanished from

the lives of Esther and her daughter. He'd gone to the West and that was the last they heard of him. Hannah was little; she soon forgot him. Although sometimes she used to have dreams about him, which she recounted to her mother. She dreamed of her father . . . Nothing could be more natural. Or maybe she dreamed of the idea of a father. Her mother would shrug. That gesture of hers was almost a nervous tic, which she passed on to Hannah: she shrugged at the drop of a hat.

—You use your shoulders to express yourself, the way most Italians express themselves with their hands, explained Johannes pedantically and at the same time glibly. Where did Richard vanish to?

—Probably the United States . . . That's what Mother said.

—Why not Germany? Maybe he had relatives here. Maybe even a wife and children . . .

Johannes was playing with fire again. Hannah pretended not to hear. If it was a joke, it was in very poor taste. The Kraut wasn't well endowed in the humor department. Not that he was much better in other departments either . . .

Her mother never remarried, but a quite elderly gentleman used to visit the house very often. He was the one who came the most frequently. Sometimes he spent the night there, in her mother's room. He was bald and his name was Nicu. Yes, that's what her mother called him. She called him "Uncle Nicu."

—That's what they called Ceaușescu too!

Now Johannes really was going too far. Hannah didn't even shrug her shoulders. Or maybe she genuinely didn't hear him, so caught up was she in her story. Ultimately, what mattered to her was to say what she had to say; Johannes's reactions were of lesser importance. But they did annoy her, sometimes. In fact, most of the time she exaggerated her annoyance. It amused her to see him take fright and want the earth to swallow him up. But wasn't he exaggerating too? A little . . .

Uncle Nicu didn't live very much longer. He'd spent a

number of years in prison. No, not under Ceaușescu, but under the other one, the one before him. Gheorghiu-Dej, that's what he was called . . . Johannes laughed. For some unknown reason. The name sounded funny to him or God knows what . . . He laughed when you least expected it, but when he ought to have laughed, when he had reason to laugh, he didn't so much as smile.

—Nicu who?

—Nicu Silbermann. He was a chess trainer. Under communism, chess was held in high esteem, even in Romania.

—I know . . . It means you must play good chess, said Johannes admiringly.

But Hannah didn't let him harbor any illusions. She didn't know how to play chess. She had no idea! She barely knew how to move the pieces. Nicu, the poor man, had tried to teach her, but didn't succeed. At first, she liked to listen to him, because he had a real knack for teaching and told her stories about emperors and empresses, knights and fools, who are lunatics who can only move obliquely, in a diagonal line. In German the fools are called runners and in English bishops. That's all she remembered about Nicu Silbermann's lessons, although to capture her interest, to attract her to that so-called game of the intellect, he'd told her everything under the sun: the pawns were the children of the king and queen, they were part of a large and united family . . . That's what she'd been told by Nicu Silbermann, whose family had been scattered to the four winds while he was in prison. They'd gone off in every direction: his wife and his children, who were already grown-ups. In chess it's rather different: the game ends when the father, the king, dies . . .

—Maybe it wasn't the best method, opined Johannes.

—You think so?

—Yes, because he left you to wallow in materiality, from which you were then unable to emerge. Or else you no longer wanted to. You daydreamed over the chessboard. After which you were no longer capable of elevating yourself to the abstract. What was worse, he prevented you from making generalizations, he inculcated in you a fear of a priori judgments, as long as he reduced everything to fairy tales. He overly encouraged the need for fairy tales, for stories.

—Fine! Fine!

—I'm sorry. I don't know whether I'm right. It seems to me too codified a game. There's too much to learn by heart. Then there's the so-called "theory of opening gambits," which isn't a theory in the least . . . I know what they say: theory is what the masters practice. That's what they say! In fact it's stupid. In other words, the theory is elaborated in the heat of practice by the great masters of the game, but for God's sake, what kind of theory is that, which . . .

—Enough! You're like a broken record!

It drove Hannah out of her wits when Johannes started theorizing, when he started on about the theory of the matchstick, as she put it. Especially since he couldn't speak without losing himself in countless parentheses. All those parentheses drove her up the wall. Sometimes she made an effort to listen to him, purely out of politeness or because she happened to be in a good mood that day. In fact, an even more plausible explanation would be that she often wanted to get something from him and was afraid to upset him, much less insult him by interrupting . . . "Self-interest wears a fez when talking to the Turk!" as her father used to say. (Which father?)

Yes, I know, you're right, Matisse painted a Romanian blouse too, but that's of no importance. In any case, it doesn't stop somebody else painting an *ie* or even lots of *ii*, if he gets it into his head. The author of the painting in question is far less famous. In fact, he's not famous at all. Maybe he will be later. After his death . . . Although the bit about death and fame isn't a foregone conclusion. It's a stupid consolation! Based on the idea of purgatory. In other words, purgatory is a place where something can still happen: the validation of a painter's work is a continuous process. But purgatory is like a tram that keeps getting more and more crowded, more and more intolerable. But we're in the middle of a rush hour, after all . . .

Was he inspired by Matisse? Why not? We find inspiration in others, we copy each other, and (pictorial?) art seems to carry on regardless. Although I'm not all that certain it does . . . Carry on where? Can't you see it's going round in a circle more than anything else? Granted, there are more and more painters; galleries are popping up like mushrooms after the rain. It doesn't occur to any of them that they should stop, throw away their paints and brushes . . . Or else they do throw them away and then use all kinds of other outlandish materials. Easel painting has been replaced by the most amazing things, but that doesn't mean that pictorial art has been renewed . . . Or the visual arts in general.

There are more and more painters, you say? And not only painters . . . Sculptors and photographers, too. Writers are also becoming more and more numerous. Readers likewise. Although there are not enough of them to satisfy the writers who are multiplying as fast as you can count and who are always complaining about how people don't read them . . . Or that they read them inadequately, that they don't understand them. But do the writers even read each other? Do they have the patience and the decency to try to understand each other?

When she returned from one of her nocturnal escapades, Hannah used to be all sweetness and light. Johannes would forget about having been upset. In any event, he avoided niggling her with all kinds of questions, which still wouldn't have served any purpose: she'd only have answered the questions it suited her to answer. If she had deigned to answer in the first place, which wasn't at all certain . . . And so Johannes wisely preferred to keep his peace and to be happy at her presence. Yes, yes, her presence! Not only her body with its creamy-white skin, which, whatever you might say, was to him an unexpected gift, but also the rest, her personality, her rather strange sense of humor, her conversation or rather the pleasure she took in narrating all kinds of events, real or imaginary. It wasn't Johannes who asked her to tell him her life story. Her past . . . It was she who wanted to! You might even say that if it had been up to him, he'd rather she'd relinquished certain confessions that brought to the fore violent memories of the kind hard to bear at the best of times, not least by the narrator. But in the present case, the narrator seemed to contradict the rule. For example, in the case of the rape, a harrowing story which she told with a certain satisfaction. A strange satisfaction! As if it gave her pleasure to rummage in that corner that any other woman in her place would have tried to forget, would have supressed, would have consigned to the depths of her subconscious . . . For, what else is the subconscious good for if not that? It was a kind of self-torture to which she subjected herself with a certain complaisance, and Johannes couldn't very well understand why. What did this masochistic recollection conceal? A psychoanalysis . . . a savage psychoanalysis? She ought to see a psychoanalyst, take treatment. Johannes mumbled something to this effect once, but she pretended not to understand. At any rate, she didn't pay any attention to his suggestion.

He looked at her closely for a few seconds and it occurred to him that the woman in front of him was quite simply reciting a part. She wasn't even looking at him, at Johannes. She was staring at some indefinite point, perhaps at a book in the bookcase or at one of the bibelots placed on the shelves in front of the books. Voltaire, Kant, Hegel . . . Or perhaps Mozart. Or why not at the miniature bust of Beethoven! The hair of the musical genius was spiky and wavy at the same time, almost curly, like Daniel's . . .

—Was that his name?

—Yes, that was his name.

—Daniel and what else?

Hannah hesitated for no more than a second.

—It's of no importance. It's of no importance what he was called. He had a German name, that is, a German-sounding name . . .

—A German name . . . A German name . . . Johannes kept repeating, in a voice that sounded more and more lost.

—Yes, but his parents had arrived from Russia at the same time as the Soviet tanks.

—That means he was Russian! exclaimed Johannes, all of a sudden perking up.

—As if that matters . . .

In truth, Johannes felt rather ridiculous. Although he hadn't wanted that story. He'd gladly have dispensed with it. In any event, he hadn't forced it out of her. But now he no longer knew how to stop her. And so he remained silent. That way, he hoped, if he didn't display curiosity of any kind, either through questions or through comments, maybe the narrator would give up and stop eventually. But once she got started, Hannah had no need of his questions. She would hesitate, she would pause, but she didn't stop. He remained silent and listened in horror. Imagine if the Sultan had been fearful of Scheherazade's stories! True, Johannes was far from being a sultan. Or a caliph . . . He'd taken off his shoes and huddled up on the sofa, with his knees to his mouth. He was waiting for the story to continue. At the same time, he was waiting for something to happen that might stop Hannah in her storytelling tracks. For somebody to ring the doorbell, Dieter for example, who never announced his visits, or the building concierge with a telegram. Or at least for the telephone to ring . . .

—At first I wasn't afraid of him, whispered Hannah and fingered her chin and cheeks, tugged her earlobe, rubbed the back of her neck. Maybe a little repulsed . . . He had a hump. He'd been left like that after a serious illness, Pott's disease or something like that . . . Among ourselves we called him the hunchback. But we were used to him. He was older than us. He'd finished lyceum a few years before and had dropped out of university. He stayed in the house most of the time. He came out only at night. Now he was keeping apart, in his corner, like a spider that has finished weaving its web, waiting. I was dancing, carefree, like the others. That was why we were there. It wasn't the first time that Dani—that's what his friends called him—had invited us to his house to dance. He had a large record player, a real piece of furniture, which he'd been sent from Israel . . . The living room was spacious, we'd rolled up the carpets, pushed the chairs against the wall, there was plenty of room. We were jigging around like the devil, we were sweating, even with the windows open it was too hot. From time to time, Rex, the huge Doberman, would bark out of the blue, or cross the room picking his way between the dancers. It was really hot! August in Bucharest is like an oven . . .

At the word "oven" Johannes gasped. But Hannah wasn't going to stop for the sake of a mere gasp. She went on with the story:

—After a while, I took off my blouse. I was now wearing just my bra. My hair was longer than it is now; it came down to my shoulder blades. And I went on dancing. I was moving my arms and hips to the beat of the latest dance hit. Daniel had loads of records. He'd never tell us about the wheeling and dealing he did to get hold of them. His parents were away. They were Party bigwigs. They had a villa outside the city, on the shore of a lake. They'd gone away for the weekend, as they say nowadays. There was no way they could have returned unexpectedly, but Dani, who had gone out of the room, came back in shouting: "They're coming! They're coming! Everybody scram! They'll be here in ten minutes!" Rex started barking his head off. We all rushed to get dressed, surprised by the turn of events, but we were full of good cheer, joking and laughing among ourselves.

"Quick! Quick!" But I couldn't find the blouse that I'd taken off just a quarter of an hour before. I was going round and round like a spinning top. "I can't leave like this," I said, "in just my bra." And the villain burst out laughing. "You're prettier like that . . ." Little did he care! "Hurry! They'll be here any moment!" My friends left, laughing and talking loudly, while I continued to look for my blouse, and I felt like crying, I was so angry. Probably somebody had picked it up and thrown it in some corner or other. Or maybe Rex was to blame . . . "Rex, come here!" But Rex couldn't talk, and so he couldn't give me an answer. I sat down in a corner, on the edge of a chair. The hunchback made his entrance, came up to me: he shuffled his feet, as if gliding over the parquet. "I can't find it," I moaned. "Never mind, why not take off your skirt too." His voice was hoarse, unrecognizable. He placed his hand on my shoulder, on my throat. A cold, moist hand. I screamed and braced myself against the back of the chair. He fell on top of me and tried to kiss me. I was struggling, trying to wrench myself away. He showed unnatural strength. I hadn't been expecting him to have so much strength. It was only then that I became afraid, when I realized that I couldn't struggle free of him, that he was much stronger than I thought. I panicked. He managed to drag me off the chair, onto the parquet floor. Then he pulled out a knife. I felt the blade, cold against my throat. Then next to my ear. I froze. With his other hand he tugged at the waistband of my skirt, ripping it. He pulled down my knickers. I helped him by lifting my bottom. Otherwise he'd have kept pulling them like a madman and it would've hurt even harder, the elastic was digging into my flesh. I was frightened, hurting, but my mind was still working, I was trying to find a way out, to find the lesser evil. He was prodding around in my vagina with his thumb. I'd have preferred his penis, because at least then he'd have done his business and gotten off me. Maybe after that he'd have let me leave . . .

Hannah paused in her story. She said:

—You can't imagine the moments of horror I went through . . .

—No . . . replied Johannes, frightened. I can't.

—The most dangerous thing is if the rapist, in his excitement, can't get it up. Then, his violence is amplified, he goes into a delirium, becomes capable of murder.

—Yes, I understand, murmured Johannes.

—The thing is, I didn't escape the thing I was afraid of. "Go on," I said, "fuck me!" That inhibited him even more. My willingness completely confounded him. He started shouting: "Rex! Rex!" The Doberman came, cheerfully wagging his tail. "Here! Come here!" The dog came up to me and started licking my belly. He had a large tongue, but it wasn't rough. The hunchback was now holding me down with the hand in which he had the knife, and with the other hand he was trying to masturbate. You understand?

—Yes, I understand . . .

—I left myself in his power. I stopped moving . . . You understand?

—Yes, I understand . . .

It wouldn't be very accurate to say that Johannes maintained her. Hannah was like a guest who prolonged her stay at the insistent pleading of the host, even though this pleading wasn't explicit, but rather part of the everyday fabric of the relationship between them. In any case, she had no scruples in that respect. Seemingly, she couldn't have cared less. As if you could know with any accuracy what's in a person's soul . . .

On his desk there was a very beautiful black lacquered box with Japanese ornamental motifs, in which at intervals he put the housekeeping money. Which doesn't mean that only Hannah did the shopping. He frequently went to the shopping center at the end of the street to make purchases, and likewise he cooked more often than she did. And so, in the box he put the shopping money, as well as pocket money for her. Johannes was generous, but thrifty. He made a note of the sums he put in the box. He also made a note of how much he spent and how much she took for her personal needs. He kept a record, you might say. I don't know what kind of a record . . . But the thing is, Hannah never overstepped the limit. Only once did she empty the box to buy herself a piece of jewelry.

—Do you like it? she asked, holding out her hand, on which glittered a ring.

Johannes liked it. He took her hand and kissed it. Then he kissed her on the mouth. On the throat. He took off her blouse, her bra. He pulled down her skirt. They made love there, on the living-room sofa . . .

Dieter was born in the GDR. He was a little boy of three or four when his parents, who worked at the GDR embassy in Paris, decided to claim political asylum. After taking that step, they went to live in the south of France, hoping that nobody would find out their address. A vain hope . . . Less than a year later, Dieter's father was murdered. The police never managed to find the murderer, although they were convinced that the former diplomat had been killed by the Stasi or even the KGB. Who knows what secrets he'd betrayed or was about to betray! He was found dead, with two bullets in his head and another two in the back of his neck.

Dieter was four or even five at the time; he'd started kindergarten and could already get by quite well in French. He liked it in that town in the Midi. Even later in life, when he spoke French, it was with a Midi accent. He'd even made friends of his own age there. He wasn't at all happy when, one fine day, his mother took him to West Berlin, where he was left in the care of an aunt, his father's sister or cousin. She'd lived there since before the building of the wall, which had separated her from the rest of her family, who remained in the eastern sector a few streets away.

It wasn't until a year later that Dieter's mother returned to Berlin. Accompanied by an American in officer's uniform: he was a colonel in the army of occupation. Another separation, another school, in a different district. The colonel tried to get the boy to like him; he gave him all kinds of presents, but without very much success. Dieter showed no liking for that adult who spoke neither German nor French, but a guttural, unintelligible language. Obviously, he learned that language later, he could hardly avoid it, but he always harbored an aversion toward it, even toward its nobler form, the English spoken, let's say, at Oxford. What's for certain is that communication between the child and the American colonel was very difficult. Dieter would have preferred to stay at his aunt's house, but the American, who in the meantime had married the child's mother, wouldn't hear of it. A child needed parents, he used to say, and a mother above all else. As far as he was concerned, he was prepared to play the rôle of father. He even insisted on adopting the boy. This was also because Frau Hammer, who by marriage had now become Mrs Colonel Sickle, was no longer able to conceive. Repeated and poorly performed abortions had placed her in that situation, which she told the American about only later, after they married, when her husband expressed his overriding wish to father a child.

—This is how I came to have an American surname, said Dieter, concluding his short and sad story. And Johannes, who sat at the same desk with him at lyceum, nodded and confessed that he was in the same situation.

—American?

—No, an orphan.

And they both burst out laughing.

As it happened, two or three years later, Dieter's stepfather, the American, died. He left the boy and his mother a vast fortune, on the condition that she never remarry. Maybe she could still have changed her surname. But she didn't. And nor did

Dieter later in life. It seemed far too complicated to him. They could have both applied to change the surname. Or to change Sickle to Sichel . . .

The telephone was ringing, more stridently than ever. He stretched out his arm to lift the receiver and already a voice, which sounded like Dieter Sickle's, was urging him to get up, to get dressed, to go outside . . . "Hurry! Hurry!" the voice whispered to him. But was it really Dieter, his friend from lyceum and then university? He wasn't at all sure. It was as if the voice wasn't Dieter's; he didn't recognize it. "Dieter!" he shouted into the receiver. "Dieter!" The other man didn't answer. Maybe it wasn't Dieter . . . But what did it matter! He felt himself being pushed from behind by an irresistible force. The voice over the telephone had been merely a kind of trigger.

He got out of bed, the door was open . . .

And who was now forcing him to run down the streets like a madman, in the direction of the wall, which wasn't far from where he lived? Who was urging him on? And why couldn't he resist? On the street there were other people, who were running too. Some were in their pajamas, like he, some were even barefoot . . . At least he'd stuffed his feet in some knackered old training shoes, but they stood him in good stead now. There were also people who had managed to get dressed, and a good job too, because the night was quite chilly. The moon had risen. A dishevelled woman in her nightshirt was running, dragging behind her a weeping child. She was barefoot. Behind her ran a panting man with a huge hammer resting on his shoulder. It was a smith's hammer. Who knows where he got it. Others were carrying picks, shovels, spades, and all kinds of other tools that might serve to demolish a wall. Otherwise, why else would they have brought them? The same as the sickle grasped in the hand of the burly man who had just darted from the dark passageway of a building from centuries ago, which had as if by miracle survived the American and British bombing raids during the war and the frenzied, poor-taste reconstruction and redevelopment of the post-war years. They were all running toward the wall . . .

He hadn't taken any tools with him—neither a hammer nor a sickle—and so he was able to run faster than the others. The wall suddenly loomed in front of him, lit up like in a theater. Who had turned on the spotlights? Who was making all those people run like rabbits? Who was conducting that spectacle of *son et lumière*? The drone of an airplane engine could be heard. Using their hammers, picks, and shovels, the people had already demolished a sizeable section of the wall. On the other side, barbed wire was visible. Not a soul was to be seen. Where were the infamous border guards?

A man had taken a cello from its case and was about to play. Or maybe it was a viola da gamba. For the time being he was just plucking the strings, he wasn't yet using the bow . . . Was he tuning the instrument?

—Rather a ridiculous dream, remarked Dieter. Completely absurd.

—Like any other dream . . . Although I don't know whether it's all that absurd. The international situation is in the throes of change. We're no longer in the Brezhnev era. Gorbachev has different ideas. You'll see . . .

—What about Honecker's ideas?

—Leave Honecker out of it! He doesn't count; he's just a lackey . . .

—Do you really think Gorbachev is planning to reunify Germany? Do you think that's what he's got in mind? Can you explain to me what's in it for the Russians for them to be so forbearing? You can't . . . You're just talking for the sake of it!

Dieter seemed a little envious. Irritated, even. Johannes looked at him and raised both arms, clenching his fists, and then snapped open his fingers: a signal urging optimism. It had been their signal of friendship since high school. Normally, the other friend was meant to repeat the gesture, after which they'd enthusiastically clap their open palms together in midair. But Dieter lifted only one arm . . . And even that was with disgust. He looked tired . . .

—Turn your back.

She obeyed, without flinching. She had large, slightly sagging breasts. When she lay on her back, her breasts spread and hung over the sides of her ribcage. Beneath one of her breasts lay hidden a mole. Johannes continued the anointment, working outward from the mole, using the same jar of honey-colored reddish-yellow substance with which he'd already anointed her back. With the palm of his hand he methodically spread the viscous substance down to her belly, to her navel. Then he worked his way back up to the breasts, causing them to quiver like mounds of gelatine. He bent down and took one of the nipples in his mouth. He sucked it, nibbled it. She laughed, slightly excited.

—Wait, you haven't finished greasing. Go lower . . .

—Lower? How much lower? he laughed.

—Don't worry, I'll tell you when to stop . . .

—Should I grease your . . . pussy?

—Whatever you think is best . . .

He'd gone to see a film, advertised in the papers as a comedy. On the poster lolled a huge parrot, or rather a multi-colored toucan, as big as an eagle. It took up about half the surface area of the poster, displaying almost every color of the rainbow. Next to the parrot and much smaller than it were four men carrying on a stretcher a woman who was laughing or crying. Hard to say which . . . The film itself was more or less the same, you couldn't say with any certainty whether it was really a comedy or whether it was something else, which made you feel like laughing and crying at the same time. Because it was impossible to decide one way or the other, Johannes was neither laughing nor crying. On the other hand, the woman in the chair next to him kept bursting into laughter every five minutes. But she didn't burst into tears . . . She was probably amazed that the filmgoer in the seat next to her remained imperturbable. She couldn't hear him laughing. And so she turned her head to get a good look at him. No, not furtively. She fixed her gaze on him for a good few seconds. Obviously, Johannes was aware of the woman's attention. Far from being perturbed, as he was, that the parrot in the film was growing as fast as the eye could see and that its living space would decrease proportionately, she was staring at him, the man next to her, so insistently that it was getting to be embarrassing. Johannes thought of moving to another seat in another row. There were plenty of empty seats! Then he looked more closely at the woman next to him, who was young, pretty . . . He therefore decided not to move, to keep manning his position. He turned to look back at the screen: a train was passing through a station without stopping, while the stationmaster respectfully and pointlessly saluted. In the windows of the carriages could be seen laughing soldiers, some of them wearing capes.

A forest stretched beside the railway line, and beyond the forest loomed a mountain, at whose base nestled the ultramodern building of a sanatorium. It was far away, out of sight, but the cinema audience knew it existed, they'd seen it in another scene, near the beginning of the film. Probably some of them had also noted the terrace where, on sunny days, the patients were wheeled out on chaises longues. Not long before, the stationmaster's wife had been admitted to the sanatorium . . . Or his daughter . . . It was quite unclear how they were related. A sad, solitary man, the stationmaster! Between trains, he went to walk in the forest, and the signalman would have to run off in search of him if the telephone rang and somebody from the central urgently had to speak to him. In those days there were no mobile telephones. Nor were there computers or the Internet. They were hard times . . .

But let's get back to the parrot. There was no doubt at all that soon it wouldn't fit in its cage. Its owner didn't seem very concerned about this eventuality. She sang in front of the mirror and combed her blond hair like Lorelei. "What is it with you and women like that!" Johannes exclaimed in his own mind and repressed a thought potentially even more misogynistic than the last one. He was annoyed. At himself! He wasn't pleased with his reaction. He didn't like it when his thoughts ran away with him without his being able to weigh them up beforehand.

The parrot kept growing, bigger and bigger, and its colors—predominantly red and yellow—seemed to be getting brighter and brighter. Even the blue, a color regarded as cold, even the blue sparkled electrically on the parrot's wings and chest.

When the woman next to him placed her hand on his thigh, Johannes first of all froze. He didn't even dare look at her. At either her or her hand. Then, after a good few seconds, he looked at the person next to him and saw she was smiling. She no longer turned her head, she no longer looked at him, she seemed absorbed in what was happening in the film, but she was smiling. On screen the parrot's owner was now lying on a bed and was being massaged or rather caressed by another woman, who, although somewhat older, closely resembled her. Their caresses were becoming bolder and bolder. The pretext was that she was greasing her body with a kind of cream or Vaseline, in any case with a viscous, reddish-yellow substance. The woman next to him was gripping his thigh with a claw-like hand. She then tried to move her hand higher. Johannes decided it was time to intervene; he couldn't let her advance recklessly like that. He covered her hand with his to halt its ascent. The woman tittered. In the film, one of the two women—in fact they were both called Maria, which didn't ease the task of the audience, some of whose members had already begun to leave the cinema—had opened the birdcage and pulled out the parrot. She cradled it in her arms like a baby that no longer had room in its cot and gently placed it on the sill of the open window. It was already bigger than a rooster. Much bigger. She took a step back to admire it. The bird was still lying curled up; in the first few moments it didn't dare do anything much. It cautiously walked from left to right, from right to left. But gradually it realized that a radical change had come over its destiny, and that it ought to take advantage of it. It puffed up its feathers. It stretched upward like a rooster, resting on its claws, which it had dug into the wooden windowsill, gripping it like a vice. It shook its feathers, puffing them up even more. And once more it spread its wings. This time it really did take flight.

Who knows how long a time had elapsed since that moment. The stationmaster grew ever sadder and more solitary. For a long time not a single train had passed through the station, which seemed to have been abandoned by passengers and the railway authorities alike. The rhythm of the film was getting slower and slower. The camera lingered on the forest, moved down a path, then another path, pausing at almost every tree. Then it would zoom in on the mountain, where it seemed to be searching for the parrot. It would return to the station, film the tracks, which had started to rust, the square behind the station, through which had passed the final convoys of people and cattle, the herds of cows and flocks of sheep abandoning the area. Behind them came carts and a few quite ramshackle vans and cars, barely crawling along.

The woman had laid her head on the shoulder of the man next to her. Johannes felt obliged to shift position: he placed his arm around the woman's shoulders and thereby her hand was now free to move up and down his thigh at will. She didn't immediately take advantage of this freedom. The parrot was flying in wide circles above the station. Threateningly? That's right: you could say it was flying threateningly. It had grown so large that its shadow looked like that of an airplane. Or maybe it was an airplane, not a parrot. And discounting the helicopter with the cameraman and director. As it was, you could hear the chirr of an engine. Which might be regarded either as a directorial oversight or as evidence of great refinement in the composition of the soundtrack . . .

A gigantic parrot runs the risk of looking unrealistic or even ridiculous. But nonetheless, the parrot in the film wasn't ridiculous. Rather it had become fearsome, no less fearsome than an eagle, for, if you saw its strong, hooked beak, what else was it, if not a multi-colored eagle . . . For quite a while, the audience had been glimpsing it from time to time, perched on the mountaintop, on a black crag, against the backdrop of which the bird's colors blazed to the full. Up above, where all that grew were a few junipers and, of course, lichens. But what audience?

The few members of the audience still remaining saw one of the Marias lying on a chaise longue on the sanatorium terrace, and they realized that in fact it was an old photograph, probably one that the stationmaster had taken out of a drawer and was contemplating with tears in his eyes. But not even this scene persuaded them to remain, to sit back down in their seats. The audience left the cinema one by one, as if copying the people from the village or town behind the station. The people in the film were also fleeing as fast as they could, abandoning the village and the station, the places where that strange and mostly unintelligible story had been unfolding. Ultimately what was there to understand? War had broken out, thought Johannes. But which war and between whom? "After all, if you like it, why do you also have to understand it?" he muttered, and the woman next to him nodded.

But what if you didn't like it?

Up until then the film had been subtitled in German. But from now on the characters' lines went untranslated. Johannes didn't understand a jot of what the characters were jabbering about. Lying on a stretcher, one of the Marias—but were there really two of them?—was being carried along a path through the forest that stretched away on the other side of the railway line. The stationmaster led the way. After a while he stopped and went behind a bush. Indiscreetly, the camera followed him, and so Johannes and the woman next to him, the only remaining members of the audience, saw him unbuttoning his flies. The others put down the stretcher and talked among themselves. The woman on the stretcher was asleep. Either that or she was pretending. When the stationmaster came back, the woman tried to get up, or at least to sit up and say something. She spoke some completely unknown language: a barbarous, guttural tongue, replete with borborygmi, while lexically, to judge by the few words Johannes managed to make out, it was a mixture of Bulgarian and Italian. Was it a Slavic or a Romance language? In vain did Johannes strain his ears, trying to divine what idiom it might be.

The woman lay back down on the stretcher. She closed her eyes. The men lifted the stretcher and set off once more. In the forest, the birds were singing their heads off: the soundtrack was reaching a climax, simultaneously emitting the louder and louder cheeping of the birds in the forest and other sounds and noises, such as the rustling of the leaves, for example, the crunching of feet on the path, the buzzing of a helicopter or motorcycles, the puffing of an old-fashioned steam engine, the laughter of men in their cups, perhaps in a tavern, whispers and sniggers, scraping and panting, maybe even music, but somewhere far away, very far away . . .

The lights came on in the cinema before the closing credits had finished rolling. Johannes stood up, likewise the woman next to him. They walked along the rows of empty seats and, holding each other tightly by the hand, they went to the exit. Johannes had parked his car not far from the cinema. He'd had the blind luck of finding a space as soon as he got there. If he hadn't found a parking space, it's certain that in the cinema he wouldn't have sat down next to Hannah, who was now climbing into his car without waiting to be asked. First they went to a restaurant.

—They were speaking Romanian, that's what it was, explained Hannah, later that evening, at Johannes's house.

—A strange language, said Johannes, rather wearied by everything that had happened to him up to then.

After they made love, Johannes took pleasure in listening to her narrate all the different adventures she'd had when she lived in Romania and after she moved to Germany. He didn't even attempt to judge how likely they were. He didn't care about that . . . That day, Hannah began to tell him, with a wealth of details, the tragicomic story of what happened to a young Englishman in a train going from Arad to Cluj, in Transylvania. The train was on its way from Budapest, in fact, and the Englishman had a slight physical handicap.

—Not a mental one, too?

—In a way, yes . . . I think you're right. Anyway, he wasn't right in the head. But you couldn't tell straightaway. What you realized more quickly was that he needed crutches to be able to get around, although he'd put them in the overhead luggage net, behind his suitcase, as if he wanted to hide them.

He was sitting by the window, reading *The Sun*. The center spread was full of naked women in provocative poses. The handicapped young man seemed very impressed by all those bared bodies. He was smacking his lips. After a while, he decided to confront the gaze of the woman opposite him, Hannah, that is, who, shortly before, had entered the compartment lugging a great big suitcase. With great strain and effort, Hannah had barely managed to heave the voluminous item of luggage up onto the overhead rack above her seat and she was probably amazed at the lack of gentility on the part of her fellow passenger, who, all the while, had been reading the newspaper rather than assisting her. Or perhaps he'd been admiring her bottom as she toiled with the suitcase. At least that much . . .

—He'd have been stupid not to, said Johannes and stroked the buttocks of the woman, who was now lying next to him on her belly, propping herself up with her elbows.

She sat down with a sigh of relief. The young Englishman shielded himself with his raised newspaper. She then looked down at his feet, at his orthopedic boots. It didn't take her long to realize that the newspaper reader sitting opposite her wouldn't have been able to assist her, no matter how eager he might have been to do so. And so in the moment when he looked at her, she smiled at him. The young man smiled back and said something in that language which, in the opinion of some, its native speakers in particular, ought, as a matter of course, to be spoken all over the world. Hannah made an effort and, drawing on her German, she understood what he was asking.

—Ann or, if you like, Annette, she answered, smiling from ear to ear.

—Mine's William. Or Double U, if you prefer . . .

—Annette is very nice, Johannes found himself saying.

The young Englishman plucked up courage. He folded up his newspaper and said something, pointing through the window at the landscape or, to be more exact, at a young lad herding three sheep. This time, the only word that Ann understood was "sheep," but she didn't catch sight of the animal in question, as the train was traveling at great speed. And so she got up to look through the window and lost her balance. She fell on top of Double U. He clutched her in arms that proved to be quite muscular. He held her to his chest and then twisted her around so that her lips were level with his mouth. He hesitated for only a second or two, in the meantime looking her straight in the eye. And he kissed her. A long kiss. She struggled in his embrace and tried to regain her balance. She fell backwards, onto the seat from which she'd risen a few minutes before. That's what you get for trying to be friendly!

"Sorry!" said the Englishman, although he didn't appear to be very sorry. His face was bright red, almost contorted: with desire, with something else . . . He stood up and, supporting himself against the window, took a step toward her. The woman moved farther back in her seat and raised her knees to her mouth. This movement revealed her thighs all the way to her bottom, and so the Englishman was able to see her black thong, or maybe he thought she wasn't even wearing any knickers. That sight caused him to lose his balance, he tottered and would have fallen on top of her if Annette hadn't unbent her legs with a powerful jerk, hitting him in the chest. After flailing his arms in every direction, the Englishman found himself back in his seat.

He stayed there for a good few seconds, during which interval Annette could have gotten up and fled the compartment, gone into the corridor to shout for help. But she didn't budge. Hannah didn't explain why, and Johannes didn't seem very desirous to find out. In that instant his desire was more than obvious and could be satisfied right there and then, right where they were, which is to say, in bed. In his impatience the philosophy teacher suddenly became brutal, which even seemed to be to the liking of the woman beside him. She allowed herself to be shoved, to be twisted around onto her back, and to have her thighs hoisted into the air in order that she might receive him.

She was sitting by the window and watching the dusk fall. The grayness thickened, it swelled like waters that kept on rising and rising . . . It had already flooded the park and was now becoming blacker and blacker: a few creatures were gliding along one side of the quadrangle gradually sinking into blackness. Strangely, the streetlamps had not yet been lit, either in the park or on the street. She leaned her elbows on the windowsill, and her forehead touched the windowpane from time to time. Then she closed her eyes.

The creatures appeared on the pavement in front of the house, where there was still a faint glow, probably from the windows of the buildings in which the electric lights had been turned on. They swung their unnaturally long arms round and round, they looked like monkeys, like chimpanzees that had just escaped from the zoo, but this impression was belied by their faces, or rather by what little could be seen of their faces, which were like those of children. Or angels.

She had a slight headache. She was experiencing that now familiar feeling, one of disgust and repulsion to do with what might be called an upset conscience, assailed by profound discontent. Put more simply: she was discontented with herself. Why did she do all the things she did? She'd have liked everything to be different or at least to behave differently thenceforward, both in general and toward Johannes in particular.

Down the street rolled a wheelchair in which a presumably disabled man was holding an umbrella illumined from within, like an electric lamp, glowing red tinted with hues of yellow. She thought that it must be the latest model of wheelchair. A few seconds later he was lost to sight, he left her field of vision. The street remained deserted.

It must be said that Johannes's dream turned out to have been a premonition, and Dieter had no choice but to acknowledge his friend was a prophet.

—You joke about it now, said Johannes, but at the time you derided me. You mocked me . . .

—I admit it! I admit it!

An event that gave rise to hope was Gorbachev's visit to Germany in May. This was after the Hungarians lifted the Iron Curtain and allowed the increasing numbers of Germans who had been pouring in from neighboring countries to travel onward to the West. Within six months, two hundred and twenty thousand citizens of the GDR had crossed to the West. At the beginning of September, the Hungarians threw open the border with Austria. It was also in that early autumn that huge demonstrations were held in Leipzig. The Germans no longer wanted to obey Honecker. A few days later, Gorbi declared (in German?): "Wer zu spät kommt, den bestraft das Leben!" He wasn't talking about the tourists, the East German citizens who had reached the border too late to be able to cross into Hungary and then on into West Germany. To leave home in the hope of eventually reaching somewhere that was still home . . . No, Gorbachev was referring to the leaders of the German Democratic Republic. At least that's what everybody, from high to low, took it to mean.

On October the 18, Honecker was replaced by Egon Krenz. The latter didn't last long. On the night between November 9 and 10, tens of thousands of Berliners massed in front of the wall and forced their way through to the other side, in a delirium of rejoicing.

She was a little disconcerted after the latest events. She went to a payphone and dialled a number. There was no answer. She dialled another number and asked to speak to Mihai. She was told that Mihai was no longer in Germany. She was unable to find out anything more than that.

As happens most of the time in such cases, Johannes didn't realize that Dieter was becoming more and more attracted to Hannah. By the time he started to have suspicions, it was too late. Although we might also think about it differently: what would he have done if he had realized earlier? Especially given that Hannah liked Dieter too. In any event, it was more than simple curiosity. She even liked his way of being, especially in comparison with Johannes: he could seem brutal, he was so direct, lacking any oratorical circumspection, aiming straight at the target. And not just in bed, where Johannes also had moments of pre-coital brutality. Unfortunately, his sexuality was short and abrupt. Johannes was emotive . . .

Dieter, on the other hand, was calm and direct; he never got emotional. She couldn't intimidate him talking about her parents being taken to Auschwitz. And even less so was she able to make him feel guilty. Granted, it hadn't been her real father who had died in the gas chambers, it had been her mother's husband . . . In fact, Dieter already knew the whole story from Johannes, and perhaps this is why he didn't allow himself to be affected by it. He'd been forewarned. He'd had time to ponder the matter, like the true philosopher he claimed to be . . . But how could he have claimed to be, when otherwise he was lucid and therefore, at least in this respect, modest . . . Modest and lucid! I don't know why, but this assessment gave him pleasure. It was like a medal he awarded himself, while looking in the mirror.

—So what if he wasn't my father! Hannah exclaimed, indignantly, but without very much conviction.

Maybe she'd grown tired of it too.

—It's more honest if you specify that detail. And also if you add that nothing serious happened to your mother . . .

—You'd think you were sorry nothing happened to her, she said, going on the counteroffensive, taking a sulky tone of voice which became more playful when she added: If something had happened to her, you would never have met me, I wouldn't be here in bed with you . . .

—Listen, said Dieter, his blue eyes gazing steadily into hers, also blue. Don't play around with that. It's not good! Even unwittingly, you contribute to devaluing the Holocaust. Understand?

She understood to a greater or lesser degree. But she nodded her head and gazed at her toes, which were sticking out from under the quilt. It was a gloomy, chilly autumn day. She pulled her feet under the quilt. Not because of the cold . . . But because she didn't like them; she found them knobbly.

She didn't say anything else; she closed her eyes.

That day, the day their story began, they'd met completely by chance, in front of a café. Dieter had a meeting with somebody called Silvio, but he'd arrived too early, and so he invited her to have a drink with him. She accepted with pleasure. Thitherto they'd only ever seen each other in the presence of Johannes. Once she'd gone with Johannes to Dieter's house. He lived in the city center, on the Kurfürstendamm. He seemed to be wealthier than his friend, although you can never know for sure what's what . . . As usual she looked at the furniture rather than the clothes. She tried to find out whether the furniture was inherited or whether it had been bought recently. That was the most important! Because if it was inherited that meant that the parents were dead and the Kraut had come into the family fortune. It was important, but not enough: they might have left him just the furniture and nothing in the bank . . . But to judge by the apartment and its central location, Dieter wasn't to be sniffed at; he was worthy of greater attention. He wasn't to be sniffed at as a man, either. He was taller than Johannes and more muscular, he had red rather than blond hair and a bristly, most handsome moustache. No, she hadn't kissed it yet, but she'd probably do so before long.

—Come up to my place one day, Dieter urged her when he saw Silvio approaching. I have to talk privately with the man who's just coming.

To be sure, he had quite a blunt manner. Some people found him impolite or even boorish. But she liked him. Or rather she'd adjusted to his way of being. And so she wasn't annoyed when he left her with the same brusqueness as when he'd invited her into the café. Especially given that he'd warned her beforehand.

She too was among those who were abandoning the village. She walked barefoot, with her head lowered, in the column of women and men. In front of them went a truck laden with all kinds of suitcases and bundles. From time to time the refugees looked up at the sky, without stopping. After a while, Hannah fell behind. She crouched at the side of the road. She was smiling. Dieter jumped out from behind some bushes. He pushed her into the ditch. None of the others turned their heads; nobody cared. The convoy went on its way, walking listlessly behind the truck. Some were barely able to lift their feet. And the sky suddenly darkened, half obscured by the eagle's wings.

At first, Hannah didn't go missing for more than two or three nights at a time. Johannes was accustomed to such absences and didn't make a big thing about it. True, he didn't know that she was spending the night in Dieter's apartment. And a good part of the day, too. But he couldn't help but feel a pang when evening approached and Hannah had still not come home. Or when he came home from the lyceum and she wasn't there. She neither left him a note nor telephoned him. The first few times, he was angry and reproached her. But her reaction to this was so violent that he abandoned further reproaches. He'd have to accept her as she was . . . Having taken this decision, he seemingly suffered less. He dined alone in the kitchen, turned on the radio—he didn't have a television and perhaps Hannah would have gone missing less if she'd been able to gaze at that enchanted window—he listened to the news bulletin, sat down at his desk and worked until late, particularly if he wasn't teaching the next day. Then he'd get ready for bed, take a sleeping pill or even two, if he was free the next morning, and go to sleep. Sometimes he masturbated thinking of her. He fell asleep happy.

One morning Johannes decided to go to Dieter's to borrow a book he knew for certain he had. They'd even talked about the book in question a few days previously. It was a translation from the French of an excellent essay about translation. Not since Schleiermacher had anybody written about the subject so profoundly. Dieter was enthused. The evening before, Johannes had telephoned him to say that he wanted to borrow the book, but he hadn't found him at home. Hannah was missing too; she hadn't been home for three or so nights. Johannes hadn't taken a sleeping pill, because he had lessons early the next morning. Furthermore, he wanted to drop in on his friend and ask to borrow the book. The next day, he was in two minds as to whether to go there before lessons and in the end he didn't. He knew that Dieter slept until late. He always timetabled his lessons for the afternoon. Nobody knew how he managed it. Only on Mondays did he have a class that started in the morning, at eleven. This is why Johannes had telephoned him: to ask whether he could drop by before nine o'clock.

He went after ten, when he had a free period. The lyceum was quite far from Dieter's apartment. He'd have to hurry. When he got off the bus on the Kurfürstendamm, just a hundred meters from Dieter's building, he thought he saw Hannah from behind. He wasn't at all sure that the woman had come out of his friend's building. He didn't run after her. And it was a good job that he didn't, because just a few seconds later Hannah jumped into a taxi that was parked nearby. And perhaps it wasn't even she, Johannes told himself, with doubt in his heart. He entered the lobby of the building in which his friend and colleague lived on the third floor and wrestled in his mind about whether or not he should ask him about Hannah. Dieter would have been apt to make fun of him. He'd always been a cynic . . . And besides, Dieter reckoned that their friendship counted for more than any woman. With that Johannes too was in agreement. And so he didn't know what to do . . . He was so caught up in his own thoughts that he pressed the wrong button in the elevator and went up to a different floor, one much higher up. He descended again by the stairs. He went up to the door of Dieter's apartment and extended his finger to ring the bell. His heart was thumping. He didn't ring. His finger came to a stop a few centimeters away from the button. He listened at the door. Maybe he wasn't home . . . Hope swelled within his ribcage. That must be it . . . If he wasn't at home, then it meant Hannah hadn't been in his apartment. But then whose?

He pressed the button and waited. From behind the door there came no sound. He rang again, holding it pressed for longer. Yes, of course. Dieter wasn't home.

Johannes turned on his heel and headed for the elevator. But maybe she had her own key, he couldn't prevent himself from thinking, and the elevator door opened without his pulling it. He stepped aside to avoid being hit by the door. From the elevator emerged Dieter, smiling from ear to ear.

—What are you doing here?

—I just dropped by, between lessons. I wanted you to lend me a book . . .

—What book?

—You know, that book about the philosophy of translation by what's-his-name . . . You were the one who told me about it. Translated from the French . . .

—Berman.

—That's it. Antoine Berman. I was curious. You said it's more interesting than the one by Benjamin.

—Is that what I said?

—Yes, that's what you said. But it doesn't matter. If you've changed your mind, it's no big deal. I still want to read it. Ultimately, translation is also a form of hermeneutics . . . It's part of my field of study, I might say.

—Let's not exaggerate, said Dieter and decided to take his key out of his pocket. The poor man's hermeneutics . . .

—I'm not the only one who says so. I've found a development to that effect in Gadamer.

—Really? In Gadamer?

—Yes, yes!

—Well, come in, what are you doing!

Johannes hesitated awkwardly. His heart had started thumping again, although not as hard as before. Why was he afraid? He could hardly find her inside. But what if he saw things belonging to her, her clothes, for example . . .

—I haven't got much time, said Johannes and looked at his watch; it was true. I can only stay a few minutes, until you find the book.

Dieter went inside first and went straight into the living room that also served as a library. There were books everywhere: in the office, in the bedroom. But he knew for a fact that the Berman book was in the living room. He went straight to the bookcase and came back just a few seconds later with the book. Johannes had barely had time to enter the hall and cast frightened glances left and right. He didn't see anything. Neither her trench coat nor her navy-blue overcoat was hanging on the rack. On the other hand, a magnificent fur coat was hanging there! It wasn't hers . . . He'd never seen her wear it. And the woman in the street he'd thought was Hannah couldn't have been her. Maybe a woman was lying in Dieter's bed right then, who, when she left, would put on that beautiful fur coat, because winter was on the way and it was getting colder and colder . . .

—What are you doing? Why are you still in the hall? said Dieter in surprise, handing him the book. Is this the book you wanted?

—Yes, this is it . . . I'll be going, I don't want to bother you.

—You're not bothering me one bit . . .

But his friend's voice rang rather false. It was obvious that he was hiding something from him. Johannes looked at him and said with a smile:

—Is she in the bedroom?

Dieter smiled back. He hadn't been expecting his friend to be so perspicacious. He then looked at the coat on the rack. He shook his head:

—She's not in the bedroom. She's gone out. She had things to do.

Johannes tucked the book under his arm and turned toward the front door. Before he went out, he took one more look at the fur coat on the rack.

For a number of minutes, Dieter hadn't said another word. He was sulking in silence. His despairing, atheistic, even apocalyptic speech, probably aimed at impressing her, a Jew from the East, now turned back on him: he felt gloomy and listless. Not even sex could tempt him. He got up to make some coffee . . .

—Tea would be better, shouted Hannah, with the quilt pulled up to her chin.

—We've run out of tea.

—Isn't there any left from last night?

—There's none left.

—Strange . . . There's really none left at all?

—None at all. There's nothing left. Why would there be anything left . . .

It had started to snow: with small, sparse flakes, which vanished within seconds of touching the ground.

She'd been living in West Berlin for a few months. She liked it, although life wasn't so calm, so pleasant as before. Berlin had been a town where young people and the elderly predominated. The adults had left for the other cities of the GFR, where they hoped to make a career for themselves, to earn money. It had been a closed, walled city, a city with no prospects, and therein had laid its charm. Now, after the wall had come down, after that momentous night, there was great agitation. People didn't know exactly what to expect. Some even talked of reunification, but most people thought it was a premature idea; the Russians would never have agreed to unification of the two Germanys. And France even less so!

One day, in the U-Bahn, she felt the presence of a man behind her; although the train wasn't very crowded, he was almost pressing up against her: she felt his thigh between her buttocks and a hand on her shoulder. She couldn't say that she disliked it, but she was curious to see what he looked like, and so she suddenly moved away, taking a step to the side and, gently pushing the attractive lady in front of her, turned her head: the man behind her was tall and well-built. He was smiling.

—Don't be afraid, he said, in Romanian.

Hannah's excitement faded. No, it wasn't Mihai, but she immediately divined whom she was dealing with. To be certain, she said between her teeth:

—*Conducătorul!*

The code word hadn't changed, despite events that not even she had dared to imagine. For the time being the new regime was still using the same men and women, who were presumed still to be loyal.

—Scornicești, whispered the burly man.[2]

—Don't be shy then, said Hannah. They need to believe we're a couple in love.

And so the man wrapped her in his long muscular arms and pulled her to him. She abandoned herself to his will. He lowered his head until his lips touched the lobe of Hannah's left ear. The Berliner woman she'd pushed a few moments before was about to complain, but on seeing the two clasped in an embrace, she changed her mind.

—I bring you good news, whispered the athletic man in Hannah's ear.

—What news?

—It's time for you to go to Paris.

—Paris?

—Yes, Paris. You're needed there.

Hannah said nothing. She thrust her hand inside the man's coat and felt there a metal object that could only be a pistol. He put up no resistance. Her fingers ran over his ribs, tickling him slightly, but he controlled himself. She rummaged further, ignored a mobile telephone and, in the other inside pocket, at last came across a wallet and a rather plump envelope. She thought that the envelope must be for her.

—I'll need some cash, she said.

—Take it.

With the dexterity of a pickpocket, she swiped the envelope and in the same movement popped it into her handbag.

—You don't seem all that delighted . . .

—Oh, yes I am! But I have to get off here.

Hannah got off the train and without looking back headed for the escalator. When she reached street level, she looked right and left, as if to get her bearings, and after two or three seconds'

2 *Conducătorul*—The Leader; Scornicești—the village of Ceaușescu's birth.—*Translator's note.*

hesitation headed in the direction of the building where Dieter lived. She wasn't at all certain that she'd find him at home. She took her mobile phone out of her handbag and rang a number. When she heard his voice her face lit up.

—And what will you do all afternoon?

—I don't know. I'll go for a walk.

—*Peripatein*, laughed Dieter and winked.

—What did you say?

—Nothing.

—What language was that?

—Ancient Greek.

—Everything was wonderful until my sister vanished. I can't have been more than six years old. I can't understand how our governess let us get out of her sight. We were both walking down the street and then one of us, I can't remember which, saw a passageway and at the end of it a patch of garden, far away, as if viewed through the wrong end of a telescope. We went toward it. Slowly. With short but determined steps. I was looking at that shard of garden and I couldn't see anything else around me. And after a while, nor could I see Sarah . . . I don't even know when I realized she'd vanished. The garden was still as far away as ever, but growing darker and darker. Dusk was falling; Sarah was no longer with me. I was now alone. I started to cry.

—Was she your twin sister? asked Dieter and pulled his chair closer to the armchair on which the beautiful Hannah was sitting, almost naked.

—Yes, I've told you that already. We were born an hour apart . . . She was born first . . .

—And her name was Sarah?

—Yes, I've already told you her name was Sarah. I don't know why you have to keep asking me the same thing a hundred times!

—No, but your friend from here is also called that, whispered Dieter, as if to himself.

—So what!

—So nothing. Carry on with the story. What happened next?

—It was terrible! I've never told Johannes what I'm about to tell you.

—Why not?

—I don't know how to explain it. I sensed that he wouldn't understand. He'd have believed me; I'm not saying he wouldn't have believed me. He believes everything I tell him. Or at least he claims to. But maybe it's nothing but convenience on his part. If not cowardice . . .

—You're more complicated than I'd have imagined, said Dieter, and Hannah didn't know what to think: was he praising her or not?

—And what did they tell you at home?

—They didn't tell me anything.

—Why not?

Hannah didn't answer straightaway. Dieter persevered.

—Didn't they ask you where your sister was?

—No.

—Not even in the days that followed?

—No.

—Didn't they tell you she'd been snatched by the Gypsies?

—By the Gypsies?

—Or by the Germans . . .

—Don't joke about it!

—No, but it's still strange. Admit it . . .

—I don't know . . . They never talked about Sarah.

That day, for the first time, they made use of the neckties they had with them. This was something that happened quite seldom; they never wore neckties even to lessons.

—It's too tight, complained Johannes, by way of explanation.

But even so, they'd agreed to her proposal. They'd both stripped naked and put on neckties. They were laughing.

—Take the belt from my trousers, said Dieter and got down on all fours.

—But mind you don't hit us with the buckle, Johannes warned her. He was shivering in a corner. His willy had shrunk and turned purple.

—Do you want to do this or not? asked Hannah, getting annoyed.

They wanted to.

A few days later, Dieter turned up with a harness, purchased from a sex shop on the Friedrichstraße. And a knout, like a dragon with multiple tongues of flame.

Perched on top of a chair, Hannah lashed the two philosophers with a fury, having allowed them to climb into bed this time. On all fours, of course.

They were in front of a bird shop, in the Adenauerplatz. It was Dieter's idea.

—I'd like to buy you a present, he said.

He was becoming more and more generous, perhaps also because he knew that before long she'd be leaving for Paris; she was dead set on it. It was unknown when she'd be coming back. If she ever came back! Hannah was wearing the silver fox fur: a Christmas present from him.

—Ceaușescu has been shot, he announced out of the blue, on Christmas Day, and placed in her arms the great big parcel, as if wishing to console her.

But Hannah had strong nerves; she didn't betray her feelings so easily. It was a magnificent fur coat! But so what! She'd seen fur coats before, her mother had even had one, albeit not one so beautiful: the foxes hadn't been silver. But she'd seen one similar in a film starring a Romanian actress who had been famous in Paris for a time. Elvira Ionescu . . . She put on the fur coat; the generous German held it for her, as proud as a toreador. It fit her perfectly! Dieter hadn't even expected it to be such a perfect fit. He walked around her, admiring it. From time to time he even let out a whistle of admiration.

—What did you do for the measurements?

—My secret!

In fact, it was very simple: he'd measured the waterproof raincoat she'd left in a corner of the hall, having gone out wearing her old, even rather threadbare overcoat. That night, Hannah was going to sleep at Johannes's place. It was his turn. And the winter looked set to be cold.

It wasn't until the end of January that she told them both that she had to go to Paris.

—What are you going to do in Paris? asked the two philosophers in dismay.

All three were in Johannes's living room. They were drinking whiskey.

She told them a long story about an aunt who had just died, bequeathing her quite a large sum. She didn't have any choice, she had to go there to deal with all the formalities, which, in France, were numerous and complicated. She wasn't the only person in the will, which was why she had to go, lest she be defrauded . . . And then there were the inheritance taxes; since she wasn't a direct successor, she'd have to pay a large sum, and no joke.

—Those French, they're a bunch of bureaucrats! said Johannes.

—I'll come with you! said Dieter.

Hannah firmly rejected this offer. She could get by very well in French and didn't need his help.

—But how will you get hold of the money for the taxes? asked Dieter.

—I'll manage . . . I'll borrow some money. There's a Jewish organization that will help me, I've got the address . . .

The two Germans nodded, filled with respect for the Jewish

organization that was prepared to assist the beautiful and intelligent Hannah. There was no longer any jealousy between them. They were like they were at lyceum once more, when they shared everything like brothers. Solidarity!

Hannah entered the bird shop first. It smelled of disinfectant, which masked the stink of the bird droppings. Which is to say, it smelled of both disinfectant and bird droppings. The perfume was a mélange . . . Dieter went straight up to the man who looked to be the owner, uttered a few hurried words, and then walked over to a birdcage in which there was a hawk or more likely an eagle chick. The label on the base of the birdcage said "Eagle from the Maritime Alps." Hannah went up to the two men, who were bantering with each other; Dieter had picked out the bird a few days previously, and the other man was in the know.

—What is it? asked Hannah.

—A parrot . . .

—A parrot?

— Of course not . . . I'm joking! It's a hawk chick. Or even an eagle chick. A present . . .

—And what am I supposed to do with it?

—I don't know. Whatever you want . . . Take it with you to Paris. As a memento of Berlin.

And Dieter's voice grew warm and tender, gurgling with hormones. For an instant Ana thought about not leaving. As if she could . . . It wasn't up to her. Dieter was carrying the birdcage with the eagle chick, pacing solemnly; he looked like a priest bearing the holy sacraments.

It was also Dieter who bought her train ticket.

Hannah didn't want to travel by night. She chose a train that left at half past eight in the morning, on the dot. She had to change at Mannheim, but it didn't matter. From there it was direct to Paris. Johannes and Dieter had taken the day off so that they could both see her off at the station. On her last night, Hannah decided to sleep over at Sarah's. It was what she wanted, and the two friends submitted without too much protest. The next day, they went in Dieter's car to the Turkish quarter, to the place that Hannah had indicated, on a street not far from what remained of the wall. Dieter had brought with him the birdcage with the eagle chick. But you shouldn't think that it was a huge cage . . . After a while, Hannah would have to buy a bigger one.

It was early. It was cold. Although snow had been forecast, it wasn't snowing. There were patches of ice on the pavement. The local residents trod fearfully; some slipped, others even fell. In fact, there weren't many people on the streets. People started work later, and not all the shops and cafés opened so early.

They came to a stop in front of a five-story building, at the number Hannah had given the night before. She hadn't arrived yet. After about a quarter of an hour, Dieter suggested they should get out of the car and try to find Sarah on the list of the building's residents. But what was her last name? And what if the apartment wasn't in her name?

—She'll miss the train, prophesied one of the two, with a certain amount of excitement, if not outright joy, in his voice. It was probably Johannes.

—Better watch your step, in case you slip . . .

Hannah suddenly appeared in front of them, but it wasn't apparent where she'd come from. She didn't seem to have come out of the building. She was positively beaming! She didn't even care about the ice. But no matter how strange it might have seemed, the wheels on her suitcase helped her keep her balance.

—Is this where Sarah lives? ventured Dieter, bolder than Johannes as usual.

At the same time, he opened the boot of the car and placed the suitcase inside. Next to the eagle chick.

Hannah shrugged and climbed inside the car. She didn't bother to answer Dieter's question. They were very late when they arrived at the station. The train was about to leave, in just two or three minutes. There they are, on the platform at last! Hannah didn't look in the least bit panicked. She strode majestically, wrapped in her silver fox-fur coat. Johannes came behind her, dragging the suitcase, while Dieter cradled the birdcage in his arms. He could just as well have held it by the handle, which is what Johannes did when he grabbed it in an excess of zeal, acting like a high-class porter: with the suitcase in one hand and the birdcage in the other, he nimbly climbed aboard the train, quickly found the right compartment, and placed the birdcage in one corner of the overhead rack, and alongside it the suitcase. Neither the one nor the other was heavy, and Hannah was a strong woman; Johannes felt a shiver down his spine. On the platform, Hannah was hugging Dieter. He was whispering in her ear that he'd come to Paris soon.

—Write to me as soon as you get there and give me your address.

She said neither that she would nor that she wouldn't. She merely nodded a couple of times.

—I ought to be boarding the train, she murmured and tore herself from Dieter's embrace. Johannes was climbing down the steps just then. He held her in his arms and said reproachfully:

—You forgot to give me your aunt's address, like you promised . . .

—I don't know it by heart. And now there isn't any time! said Hannah, getting annoyed.

—Write to me as soon as you get there.

—Yes, yes . . .

Hannah hurried up the steps of the train carriage. In a hurry, not paying attention, she trod on the hem of her fur coat and fell on one knee. A man's arm helped her pick herself up. She looked up and her eyes met those of a large man whose forehead was made to look all the higher because of a receding hairline.

—Hannah! Hannah! shouted the two philosophy teachers left behind on the platform.

They were both dressed the same, wearing leather overcoats, probably with a lining. They looked like they were out of some 1950s Soviet film, in which two men wearing leather coats on the platform of a train station in Berlin could be nothing other than Gestapo agents. They both held their right arms raised, to attract her attention or to salute her . . .

She half turned around and waved at them. Her other hand was still in the capacious grasp of the man, who was looking in amusement at the two men left behind. Just a few seconds later, the train set in motion; the door of the carriage closed automatically. Hannah turned around and made her way down the corridor. She quickly reached the compartment where she had a reserved seat. She went inside and, after a slight hesitation, went to the window. She opened it. Far behind on the platform, the two men who had accompanied her to the station, after taking tender and solicitous care of her throughout her sojourn in Berlin, were still waving her farewell. But their arms were moving more and more slowly. And she saw them become smaller and smaller, more and more insignificant . . .

She pushed the window shut. She looked at her suitcase, which was on the overhead rack, where Johannes had put it, she took off her fur coat, hung it on the peg by the window, sat down, and breathed a sigh of relief: Alone at last! She stretched out her legs. How about she took off those wretched boots that were pinching her feet . . . Then she remembered the eagle and looked to see where the birdcage was. At that very moment the door to the compartment opened and the large man appeared.

—May I?

He had a deep voice, a baritone verging on a bass. And he was also a little hoarse. At first they talked about the weather.

—In France it's warmer than in Germany.

—Really? Why is that?

—Because it's nearer the ocean. In Paris, for example, it almost never snows. And if it does snow, it melts the next day.

—A pity . . .

—When it snows, the Parisians are overjoyed, especially the children, but also troubled . . .

—But why?

—Not even they know why . . . They're afraid their cars might get stuck in the snow. And sometimes they do. Not in Paris, obviously . . . On the outskirts. In the greater Parisian area. In the Île de France. There are also regions of France that have heavy snowfalls and no joke! Not only in the mountains. Especially in the center of the country, where the climate is continental.

The large man seemed to know France very well.

—Interesting, she said, and thought that in the end she ought to take her boots off. It was getting hotter and hotter in the compartment . . .

—Have you been to Paris before? he asked and finally looked at the birdcage.

To be more precise, he stood up and, since he was tall, his head came level with the birdcage. He looked at the eagle chick for no more than two or three seconds. Politely, he turned his head to hear her answer.

—No, I haven't.

—It's the most beautiful city in the world. More beautiful than Vienna or London. Not even Rome can compare with Paris! As for this Berlin of ours, what can I say? Maybe now it will start to become more attractive, to acquire a bit of color. But first we need to get rid of the wall. We need to continue demolishing it . . . Are you a Berliner?

—No, obviously not. I thought it was obvious from my accent.

The man sat back down on the bench seat, which was upholstered in a bluish-green velvet-like material. He looked closely at the woman opposite him. For a good few seconds.

—Maybe you're Swedish? Or Norwegian? I had a Norwegian friend, a very beautiful woman, almost as beautiful as you . . .

But she was blond . . .

—You're too kind . . . I'm not Swedish. Nor am I Norwegian.

—Then you must be Hungarian. Why didn't I think of it!

—Nor am I Hungarian. I'm from Eastern Europe.

—Polish then . . . Or maybe Bulgarian . . .

—You guessed wrongly. I'm from Romania . . .

—From Romania . . . Formidable! La belle roumaine! Of course! You look just like that actress who found fame in Paris. Just a moment, let me remember her name . . .

—Elvire Ionesco?

—Exactly! Ionesco . . . Maybe the wife of the playwright . . .

—Of Eugène Ionesco?

—Or his daughter . . . Yes, yes. That's what I heard . . .

—His daughter? Impossible . . . Elvire Ionesco was older than the playwright. And if I'm not mistaken she's dead.

—She's dead? Then maybe she was a cousin . . . They had the same surname, after all.

—Romania is full of Ionescus!

The man opposite her fell silent. He suddenly became gloomy, as if the beautiful Romanian woman's statement had deeply saddened him.

—You know, Ionescu comes from Ion, which is the same as Johann, Johannes . . .

The admirer of the playwright and of Paris wearily shook his head and closed his eyes. Hannah hesitated for a few moments, and then she bent down and took off her boots. One of the boots fell and made a noise, which woke the man, who was asleep, or perhaps not . . .

She was worried about Mihai. She hadn't seen him for almost two months. The day before, she'd waited for him at Mehmet's, but he hadn't shown up. Eventually he called to say he wouldn't be coming.

—I miss you, she said over the telephone.

—Never mind, we'll see each other in Paris.

She consoled herself in the arms of Mehmet all night long. The next morning, she was barely able to wake up. Mehmet picked her up and carried her to the shower.

—You'll miss the train, he said. He made her some strong, bitter Turkish coffee, and finally he got her back on her feet.

In Mannheim she had to change trains. She had plenty of time: almost twenty minutes.

Wolfgang was delighted to carry the birdcage. Or so he said. He had only a briefcase, and so he carried her suitcase too. They easily found the other train: a kind of TGV, which made no stops until Paris. They took their seats in another first-class compartment, just the two of them.

—And the eagle, added Wolfgang.

She'd told him that her name was Annette. From Anne, obviously. Ana, in Romanian. Or Aneta . . .

—Annette is a very nice name. The French brought it to Berlin. The Huguenots!

Annette knew who the Huguenots were. She'd read *La Reine Margot*. In French.

—You're all French speakers in Romania, said Wolfgang admiringly.

—That was in the old days. My parents' generation were French speakers. Or rather the rich were, those educated in Paris, the intellectuals. The Romanians have become Americanophiles. And English speakers . . . For years and years they waited for the Americans to save them from the communists. Even if they'd crawled on their hands and knees, they ought to have gotten here by now, as my poor father used to say. Wolfgang liked her words, but he didn't say anything.

They both seemed full of good cheer. Annette looked out of the window for a few seconds and saw a young man in a wheelchair, who was probably waiting for somebody. He was very agitated. He kept looking all around, jerking the wheelchair left and right with very great skill.

Wolfgang was saying something about accidents: there were more road accidents than airplane accidents.

—It may well be, said Annette, or Ana, as her father used to call her . . . It may well be, but in a car accident you have a greater chance of surviving . . .

—You survive, said the large, wise Wolfgang, but in what state? In a wheelchair, mutilated to the end of your life, disfigured . . . You'd be better off dead!

—Better red than dead, she quipped, and they both laughed.

The train set in motion. It picked up speed. After just a few minutes it reached top speed.

—It's not only fear of an accident, Ana went on. She also took the train because she liked traveling by train. Trains are more comfortable than traveling by car . . .

—That's true . . .

—Not to mention by plane: you sit there cramped, unable to move from your seat; you have no more space than a hen in some ultramodern factory farm, like the one I saw near Berlin, in Wannsee . . . In a train it's different! You've got room to move around, you can go out into the corridor, and when you look out of the window you have things to see. Traveling by train is human, natural . . . Humans weren't made to fly!

—Are you really so sure?

There was a pause in the conversation. Ana thought about Mihai once more. He'd promised they'd see each other in Paris. But she didn't put much faith in his promises. True, it wasn't up to him. Who knows where he was now . . . In what out-of-the-way places! She looked out of the window: the landscape was rather ordinary and monotonous. The man opposite took up the conversation once more, still talking about accidents. About accidents and children's apparent unconcern when it came to accidents and their eventuality. She didn't really agree with him, but she refrained from contradicting him. She preferred to bring the subject round to childhood, her childhood, which had been the happiest time of her life. Wolfgang nodded. Was it for him too?

—Yes . . . of course . . . Childhood . . .

A childhood that had been brought to an end by a dreadful event: her twin sister had been kidnapped by a pedophile, who raped and then killed her.

—During the time of Ceaușescu?

—No, not long before, during the time of Gheorghiu-Dej.

—Too little is known about that period . . .

—What do you mean?

—Not much has been written about it . . . Not then and even less so now. The people who lived in that period avoid talking about it. I mean the ones who left Romania . . . I don't know why. Probably they're afraid . . . But of what? Of whom?

—Is that what you think?

—I'm not just talking about Romanians. Nor do the Germans or the Jews who managed to leave the country. With the help of the German or the Israeli state and various international Zionist organizations. Which had to pay large sums for them . . . It now looks like the situation will change considerably, above all there, inside the country . . .

Ana closed her eyes. She listened to the German's words and thought of her tempestuous and rather pointless life.

III

She'd barely slept; she was exhausted. She had to drink a coffee no matter what. She had to warm up a little, to rest. Her back was aching. She decided to go inside the first café she came to. Maybe it was no more than simple chance. At the time she had no reason to think of fate. It wasn't until much later . . . Until too late, that is . . .

She hesitated for an instant, and then opened the door, entered, and went over to a table by the coatrack—the table was in an excellent position: neither too near the glass front of the café, nor too far away. She plonked her handbag on a seat, then she took off her fur coat, standing on tiptoes to hang it up. She knew that in making that movement her body would arch like a bow and present the males in the café with a very advantageous view, also enhanced, of course, by her dungarees, made from a material that was probably a mix of artificial fibres, but also contained a little silk. She had bought them before leaving Berlin. No more than two weeks had elapsed since then.

There were not many people in the café. At a nearby table, a man with glasses kept staring at her, instead of reading his newspaper. On the page of the newspaper visible to her she could see the head of a horse wearing blinkers, like the horses from her childhood in Romania, the horses that pulled hearses. True, the horses that pulled hearses were fancier, bedizened with all kinds of black and violet ribbons, and they wore cornets on their ears. She later discovered that the leather blinkers, which were also called "horse glasses," were highly necessary for those skittish animals, whether they were running over the turf of the race track or whether they were moving at a walk to the cemetery. The hearse had pulled up in front of Colonel Poenaru's house. The colonel's mother had died, and the grandchildren, a boy and a girl, had gone to the gate and shouted at the top of their lungs to her and her sister Maria:

—We've got a dead body! We've got a dead body!

When the café owner came over to take her order, she was smiling at her memories of childhood, her gaze was turned toward the past, and she didn't even notice that the man had been standing there patiently for a good few seconds. She ordered a coffee.

Jean-Jacques was also the owner of the café. The beautiful stranger had made an impression on him at the very first sight. First there was the majestic entrance of the woman wearing the silver fox-fur coat, and then there was the way in which she hung up the fur coat, her body, her steatopygous bottom, and her golden blond hair . . . She looked like those actresses from before the war, maybe even Elvire Popesco, whom he'd seen in his youth; he'd admired her at the theater and the cinema. She was beautiful, elegant; she was distant. That was how a genuinely elegant woman should carry herself: she should keep herself at a distance. He'd never had a genuinely elegant woman.

He retracted the coffee cup from beneath the filter, he placed it on the tray, he added the sugar dispenser and a glass of water, and with measured gait he went to the table of the woman, who this time saw him coming and smiled benevolently.

Ana had grown accustomed to Jean-Jacques's café. After taking off her fur coat, she sat down at the same table as the day before and from her handbag she took the book she'd just bought and started leafing through it. Jean-Jacques approached the table, taking short steps, in no hurry. Strictly speaking, he might have waited for a signal on her part, as was fitting and as he was otherwise in the habit of doing: he'd leave the customer to look around for two or three minutes, to think about what he wanted to drink, to decide. True, she was reading rather than looking around and she didn't give the impression of being stuck for choice, since she always asked for the same thing: a coffee.

The beautiful stranger lifted her eyes from her book and looked at him. He quickened his steps.

—A coffee, please!

Even her voice resembled the actress's, Jean-Jacques said to himself. She has the same East European accent. No, it wasn't an Italian accent. He knew the Italian accent very well. To force her to say a few more words, he asked:

—An espresso?

—Yes, yes, an espresso.

—Short?

—Yes, short . . .

Although it wasn't possible to say that they'd engaged in a discussion, he was nonetheless delighted that they'd exchanged a few words. Jean-Jacques was irremediably shy. Especially with women.

Ana had closed her book and was now looking in the direction of the bar. The barman had his back turned, he was tinkering with the filter machine, preparing the coffee she'd ordered. He was a large man, who might be said to look older than he really was. He also had an assistant, Ed, a rather plump young man, who didn't look older than twenty. But perhaps he was older, thought Ana and gave him one of her sweetest smiles. Indeed, a languorous smile . . . Usually, Ed came only at lunchtime, when the café proprietor couldn't cope on his own. That day he'd come earlier, however.

—I'm serving the lady! shouted Jean-Jacques when he saw Ed about to go over to the woman.

That day, Ana was wearing not her silk dungarees, but a short skirt that revealed her knees and half her thighs. True, she was also wearing dark-colored stockings, which rather attenuated the effect. Her table was in full view of the bar. Because he didn't dare gaze at her steadily, the barman cast her quick, sidelong glances.

She came almost every day, but she never stayed for more than half an hour. She always sat at the same table. Not even she knew why. And the table was always free. Probably the café owner made sure that nobody else sat at that table, at least not before she came.

—Don't sit there. That table is reserved.

The customer looked slightly confused. He was holding a racing paper, *Paris-Turf*, let's say. Open at the page reserved for the *tiercé*.

—Reserved?

—Yes, yes. Don't insist.

—Well, then put a reserved sign there, a label, something. If it's reserved, at least let us know . . .

She ordered a coffee with a drop of milk, and sometimes a croissant. She had a grave voice and an accent that Jean-Jacques was unable to identify immediately. It might have been an Italian accent, but the café owner knew the Italian accent well. And he sighed. If only he had never come to know it! No, it wasn't an Italian accent, but rather a Slavic accent. Although he wasn't certain even of that. She had the same accent as Elvire Popesco! That was it! She only imitated a Slavic accent, although it wasn't very clear in his mind why a woman from Romania would have needed to imitate a Slavic accent, a Russian one to be precise . . . Anyway, for Elvire Popesco it was understandable; you could construct a number of hypotheses in an attempt to explain it. Ultimately, she was in theater . . . She was an actress! In addition, she probably felt humiliated that her country meant more or less nothing in the eyes of the French. The same thing might be true of the beautiful stranger. There's a little bit of the actor in all of us, especially when we are in a foreign country. It's as if we were playing a rôle or had a mission to complete . . .

When, after an absence of a number of days, Yegor finally reappeared, Jean-Jacques asked him what had happened for him not to have come the day before or the day before that . . .

—I was busy, answered Yegor, surprised at his friend's indiscreetness and insistence.

He sensed he was agitated, anguished, even. His face was tired, upset; his eyes were bloodshot, probably from a lack of sleep.

—Let's hope she'll come today . . .

—Let's hope who will come?

—You'll see . . .

—Stop being so mysterious and fix me a vodka. Put it in a bigger glass. Yes, yes! A double.

Jean-Jacques knew Yegor's exigent demands very well, but he was still reluctant to serve him vodka in a whiskey glass.

—Every drink has a specific kind of glass, he grumbled as he looked for a recipient more to Yegor's taste.

—Don't you start on at me like Madame Renard . . . The customer is king!

—Yes, Your Majesty . . .

—Every customer has his foibles. I drink a small glass in one gulp. Understand? I knock it back! A larger glass allows me to drink more slowly, to savor it. Today I feel like savoring it.

—As you wish . . . Wait! Look, she's coming in!

—Who, brother? Who's coming in?

—Turn around and you'll see how magnificent she is!

Ana entered the café and without a moment's hesitation went to the table at which nobody had been bold enough to sit. She took off her fur coat, hung it on the coatrack, stretching her body to the highest peg, turned around, cast a quick glance at the bar, where the two men were standing with their heads almost pressed together as they gazed at her, admired her. She granted them half a smile and at the same time sat down and took a book out of her handbag.

—A coffee and a glass of water, she said, without raising her voice, and Jean-Jacques read her lips.

There was no need for him to hear her words . . . He'd already turned his back, ready to manipulate the coffee machine, which thus allowed Yegor to give the woman a winning smile. Far from being daunted, the woman turned to him and flashed her teeth, which were almost as white as you would find in an advertisement for some brand of toothpaste or other. The racetrack punter, who was watching the scene, also smiled, but into empty space, since nobody was looking at him. I admit that this last statement, being peremptory, is rather risky and might give rise to controversy, but now isn't the moment for such stale theoretical parentheses.

She liked to ride the underground train. It made no impression on her that sometimes she was dozens of meters below ground. Nor that an earthquake could cause a very serious accident. For example in Bucharest, which, as is well known, lies in an area of violent seismic activity. In Berlin, Dieter had told her one day:

—Maybe you were a mole in a past life.

—*Une taupe!* she thought to herself now, translating the word into French and beaming from ear to ear.

The man sitting opposite her, who was pretending to read a book, thought the smile was meant for him and smiled back. The Métro train had just left the Stalingrad station, and it struck her that almost all men were prone to megalomania. And she smiled again.

—Where are you getting off?

—Wherever you want to get off, she answered and was barely able to stop herself from bursting into laughter.

She went to have her hair dyed just two days after she arrived in Paris. She entered a hair salon near the rather modest hôtel where she was staying. In vain had she hoped that Wolfgang would take her under his protective wing. Before the train entered the Gare de l'Est, he tore a page out of a notebook and wrote down a telephone number where he could be reached. She was unable to do the same and tried to explain why: she didn't yet know where she'd be living. But he was in a hurry or, in fact, wasn't particularly interested.

—Yes, very good, said Wolfgang. Very good . . .

On the platform a tall man in a leather coat was waiting for him, with an Alsatian on a leash. The dog's muzzle made it look even more fearsome.

—I'm sick of this hair color . . .

The hairdresser, who can't have been more than nineteen or twenty, asked what color she'd like. She shrugged and looked in the mirror at the hairdresser, who had matte skin and black hair, which glinted red in places. She'd probably washed it with henna. Then she looked at her own hair, which had been dyed black since she was in Czechoslovakia. She raised her eyebrows, her eyes boggling with indecision. The girl then vanished without saying a word and came back with an album full of samples: locks of hair dyed all kinds of colors, from Japanese glossy black to Finnish flaxen blond. There were also locks of hair that were gray, a salt-and-pepper mixture, stark white, silver, locks that had hints of blue or even pink. Among them she also saw a blue and a green lock of hair.

—I'd like to have hair like Elvire Ionesco, whispered Ana.

—I'm sorry, I don't understand . . .

—Like Elvire Ionesco, the actress.

—I don't know her, said the hairdresser haughtily. What films has she been in?

Ana shrugged. She couldn't remember any of her films. Had she ever seen her in a film? She remembered her conversation in the train with Wolfgang, who told her she looked like Elvire Ionesco, the playwright's cousin. But naturally, the hairdresser couldn't have known that.

—She had blue eyes. Like me, said Ana, and the young woman from North Africa leaned closer to the mirror to look at her eyes.

—Doesn't she appear in films anymore?

—I think she died, said Ana. She's definitely dead. She was murdered . . .

—A long time ago? asked the hairdresser, with sympathy.

—I don't know . . . I wasn't in France at the time.

—Where are you from?

—Berlin.

—The men here prefer blonds, declared the hairdresser and looked at the mirror to see what effect her words had had.

It was a unisex salon. But most of the customers were women. A man who was just about to leave gave Ana a very interested look. No, he didn't wink at her. It's not true. A lot of the time she thought that men were winking at her. But it wasn't always true. The man went to the door, accompanied by the barber who had just cut his hair. He paused with his hand on the doorknob and turned his head. Yes, this time he really did wink at her and gave her a complicit smile. Why complicit? Ana shrugged her shoulders, vaguely annoyed.

She was unable to remain at the hôtel because of the eagle chick. The black man at reception had looked askance at the birdcage.

—Is that really an eagle?

—An eagle chick.

—What do you feed it?

—Human flesh, she answered. Corpses . . .

The black man gave a somewhat frightened look, and then he laughed. Let's say he had a sense of humor, but what attitude would the others take, in particular the owner of the hôtel, who had in any case been informed and had probably even gone up to her room to take a look at the bird? What is more, as he looked at the bird, he'd been tempted to place the birdcage on the windowsill, to open the window and then the cage. She really had to find a small apartment in a quiet, well-off neighborhood . . .

—Have you decided?

The hairdresser had begun to lose patience.

—Blond! I want to be blond, like the actresses before the war. A platinum blond . . .

—It's gone out of fashion, the girl behind her pointed out.

—It doesn't matter.

—Show me what shade you're interested in, please. This one?

—Yes. In fact no, this one! Or this one . . .

—Whichever you like, it's all the same to me!

—But which one do you like?

—Like I said, platinum blond isn't fashionable anymore. Better this Venetian blond . . .

—I've never been to Venice, sighed Ana and looked in the mirror.

At the rear of the salon, in the farthest corner, a very corpulent man, with a face covered in shaving foam, was shifting uneasily in the barber's chair. The barber had placed a towel as big as a tablecloth around his throat and was brandishing a razor as big as a scimitar . . .

—Me neither . . .

—But you still have time. You're young. You have so many years ahead of you. Are you married?

—Married? said the girl in amazement, as if it was completely unheard of.

—Yes, married. At your age I'd been married for two years already. To an aviator.

—An aviator?

—Yes, an aviator. A long-distance pilot. He flew above the oceans . . .

—Was he French?

—No, mademoiselle! He wasn't French . . .

But before she could divulge the nationality of the long-distance pilot to whom she'd been married, she saw the large man half rise from his seat and heard him scream:

—No, not with the cutthroat razor!

How about that, thought Ana: in a Parisian hairdressing salon where they tell you straight out that platinum blond is out of fashion, they still shave people with a cutthroat razor.

And what a razor!

—They're not all French, quipped the hairdresser.

Probably she didn't hear the screams and then the muffled groans of the customer at the back of the salon, she couldn't see what was happening there: naturally, since she had her back turned and would have had to bend down to see it in the mirror. Two men and a woman had piled onto the poor customer, they'd probably stuffed a napkin in his mouth, and now, using a hemp rope, but which was dyed blue, they were binding him tightly to the barbershop chair, which seemed to be bigger than all the other chairs in the salon. Ana realized that she had no choice. She had chanced upon an establishment that was none too orthodox . . . The wisest thing to do would be not to ask any questions, to act as if nothing had happened . . . To give up wishing to look like the actress, to accept without further discussion whatever color she was offered, to allow herself to be dyed come what may, even be it green or blue, but to have done with it already . . . How stupid she'd been to come into that unfamiliar hairdresser's, where no end of things went on.

—You choose the color, said Ana in a small, thin voice.

And she closed her eyes.

—I think, said the young hairdresser very calmly, that the color best suited to your eyes and skin, since the skin counts too, would be a platinum blond, you know, like the color actresses before the war used to have . . . There's a television channel that shows nothing but films from before the war. Some of them are funny. Like those films with Jean Gabin when he was young. What a cool guy! That was a man, and no joke . . . All the actresses swooned over him. Even Marlene Dietrich, that German who fled in fear of Hitler, because he kept making her proposals. There's even a rumor that she was forced to do the business with him, so that she could obtain the documents to leave the country. She got on a plane and never went back! She really stuck it to the man with the moustache. Marlene went to America, to see that other man with a moustache, Charlie Chaplin. But it wasn't there that she met Jean Gabin. To tell the truth, I don't know where it was. I flicked through her biography once, but I can't remember. It wasn't my book . . . So . . . That's what I think. It's a very good thing that you're leaving it up to me. The boss says I'm very talented. I don't know whether he means it or not, but that doesn't matter. All right, I'll go and get everything I need and I'll be right back . . . Right away . . .

How old could she have been when her father used to wait for her in the little park by the lyceum? She can't have been more than eleven or twelve. In fact, there was no longer even any need for him to come and pick her up from school, as it wasn't far from where they lived. It was two bus stops away and so she could walk the distance; she only took the bus if it was raining or if she was late. Because she was embarrassed in front of her schoolmates, her father agreed not to show himself except at the bus stop, and even so, only as if he'd just happened to be passing . . . True, he didn't always come. Sometimes, she'd look behind her to see if he was following her. And when she passed the park, she'd look out of the corner of her eye and she didn't always see him. In time, she glimpsed him more and more seldom. After a while, she didn't glimpse him at all. They'd thrown him in prison. When he was released, she was in her last year of lyceum. And he'd aged very badly.

Ana had finished her coffee, but she was still there, sitting at the table, with a book open in front of her. But she wasn't reading, or in any event she'd long since stopped turning the pages. She was staring into space. Her mind was probably elsewhere, in Germany . . .

Before meeting Johannes in that cinema (what was the film called? She'd forgotten), she'd lived not far from the wall, in a mostly Turkish neighborhood. Mihai had set her up there when they both arrived from the GDR, albeit via Czechoslovakia. Clandestinely, it would seem. After the fall of the wall, they'd both obtained a kind of *Ausweiß*, but which wasn't much use. She could get by in German quite well. Anyway, she spoke the language better than many Turks, who were either recent immigrants or had little contact with the German population and who knew only enough to get by at work, where they never had to say more than hello, or in the few shops that weren't owned by Turks like themselves. The Germans didn't much like to live near the wall. Near that concrete and barbed wire bastion, you found mostly Turks and poor Germans. And all kinds of outsiders, artists, political protesters, anarchists, people from various categories attracted by the wall or, rather, indifferent to it. Because of the wall, rent and the price of food and clothing were obviously much lower. And so that was the main reason why so many people settled there.

Ana lived in a run-down building, in a shared apartment. Next to her room, which was slightly larger than the others, was Mehmet's room, "my cell," as he used to say in an attempt to make her feel sorry for him and ultimately in order to seduce her. It's by no means certain that the size of the Turk's den was what persuaded her to sleep with him . . . What's for sure is that after they made love, she used to send him back to his own room.

Mehmet was a likeable man. Trustworthy, too. Or to be exact, she could trust him. Even if he seemed a little daft, with his head in the clouds. He had all kinds of strange ideas.

—Because of the seasons and the calendar, he used to say, we spend our lives going round in a circle.

—Then what ought to happen instead?

—I don't know . . . In fact, it's very good the way it is, he added, after thinking about it a little. It's like music . . .

—What's like music?

—Life . . .

Nedim lived on the same corridor with his mother and sister.

Nedim was a young man of around twenty or twenty-two, who dreamed of becoming a singer. For hours on end he used to mangle music on his guitar, driving all the other residents out of their wits. You could hear him throughout the building, which had three floors and a kind of mansard. Nedim's father had been a bricklayer and had died in an accident at work. The scaffolding he and two other workers were standing on collapsed. His widow and children lived on welfare from the German state.

There was only one native German living in that tenement block in Kreuzberg: under the rafters, in a kind of mansard, albeit one that was long and broad, stretching for the entire length of the building. The mansard was in fact an attic and was only partly furnished, according to Nedim, the only one who had been privileged enough to visit the hirsute old man, but dozens of square meters of which were heaped with dusty books, stacks of paper and files. Herr Schlesak lived up there like an owl. The people on the top floor could hear him moving around all night long. He left his attic only seldom, and nobody could swear that they'd ever seen him descend the stairs. Nedim bought him what he needed, and once a month the postman would climb the stairs to his attic, grumbling, to deliver his pension or some other monthly income. Some said that in fact he was the owner of the whole building.

—He comes out only at night, idle tongues said.

—But when? And why don't we see him?

—He doesn't need to go out of the door, to descend the stairs, Nedim said with a smile. The others, the young people of Nedim's age and even others, people in middle age, who out of curiosity flocked to listen to what he said, didn't understand what he meant at first.

—Don't listen to him. He talks nothing but nonsense, Nedim's mother would interject, if she happened to be there.

—Tell us! Tell us! pleaded the others.

—Well, he opens the window . . . and here Nedim paused,

waiting for the others finally to understand what he meant.

—He goes out of the window? asked the curious listeners in horror.

—Like a bat, like a giant bat he flies away into the night . . .

—Why should I be responsible for my ancestors? Or even for my parents? asked Dieter, defensively. Legal and even moral responsibility has to be confined to the individual, otherwise we regress, we find ourselves subject to the *lex talionis* once more, a yoke that the individual is no longer accustomed to bear. Wasn't there a trial in Nuremberg? The guilty were tried and punished. You can't incriminate an entire people, generation after generation. You're liable to succumb to the same idiotic obsession as those representatives of Christianity who for centuries continued to blame the Jews for the killing of Christ.

She could have told him that it wasn't certain that Jesus was exactly the person he was believed to be . . . But anyway, Dieter didn't believe, he didn't believe in him one bit! But she didn't say anything. She stretched in a languid, conciliatory way. One of her breasts came level with his mouth, and without a moment's hesitation his lips battened onto it.

Jean-Jacques had a real weakness for people from the East, especially Russians. He'd befriended Yegor quite quickly, even though the Russian seemed to love alcohol more than the barman thought was advisable. It's strange that among bistro and café proprietors, among barmen and waiters, one can find some of the most determined adversaries of drinking to excess. Or maybe the daily spectacle of drink-induced human degradation was stronger, more convincing than economic interest, which they didn't think about in any direct or concrete way. Nor did Jean-Jacques like alcoholics, drinkers who got drunk quickly and were eager to cause a scene. Yegor was a drinker—and a vodka drinker at that—but the thing is, he didn't get drunk.

At any rate, he didn't get drunk quickly. This is what he'd tried to explain to Madame Renard, the owner of the tavern by the Métro station, whom he'd left for Jean-Jacques. Yegor got drunk only very seldom, and only at home, drinking straight out of the vodka bottle. He'd drink alone, and sigh. He didn't turn on the television set or the radio. And then, he'd really get drunk. Sometimes he'd cry. The tears streamed slowly down his cheeks. He'd stare blankly up at one corner of the room, without seeing anything. Or up at the ceiling. The light fitting on the ceiling would start to go round and round, and even the photographs he'd pinned up in one corner of the room, above the chest of drawers and the bookshelf, would swim around alarmingly. Yegor would stretch out on the bed, he'd prop himself up on one elbow, swig the dregs left at the bottom of the vodka bottle, and close his eyes. The room would be swaying like a ship on the waves. Soon, Yegor would be asleep, snoring. Sometimes he talked in his sleep. In Russian, obviously.

—We don't serve persons in a state of inebriation, declared Madame Renard, thinking of her son, dead from cirrhosis.

—But dear lady, I'm not drunk. I'm perfectly sober. In any case, your glasses are so small that you can't even taste the drink. Don't make me laugh . . . How do you expect me to get drunk drinking from a thimble!

—If you don't like my glasses, then beat it! Go and drink somewhere else!

And that's just what Yegor did: he left Madame Renard and went to Jean-Jacques's café, which he'd entered only once before, a few months previously, after he moved to the neighborhood. Before that he'd lived in the north of Paris, somewhere near the Place de la Bataille-de-Stalingrad.

—The French are the last admirers of Stalin! In no other country in the world can you find his name nailed to plaques on the buildings.

—We're hardly going to change our street names to suit

dictates from abroad, said Jean-Jacques defensively, and he gave a satisfied laugh, not even he knew why. Maybe he imagined he'd made a joke.

—They oughtn't to have named a street after a tyrant in the first place. That's what you call the cult of personality. Stalin was still alive when you put up that plaque . . .

—The Communist Party put it up . . . Party members demanded it. There was all that enthusiasm after the war, after liberation. The People's Front didn't have time to take such initiatives before the war. Granted, Stalin was held in high esteem, but so much so that . . . And Stalingrad wasn't yet the heroic city it became later.

—Why not name a street after Hitler?

—To you it's the same thing?

—Before the war nobody would have thought of doing that: naming a street after Hitler. And the French pro-Nazis had had the decency to wait and see whether Hitler won the war . . . I think that not even in Germany was there a street named after Hitler . . .

—Not even in Germany? said Jean-Jacques in amazement.

—I don't know. I don't think so . . . In any case, after the war, they'd still have changed the name, wouldn't they?

—You're right about that!

—Then why didn't you do the same with Stalin? Stalingrad Square, Stalingrad Métro station . . . Paris is the only city in the world where the name Stalin sits there nicely on the walls of buildings and on the Métro map. Children learn the name as soon as they can read; they utter it without knowing what it means. And the argument that the name is that of a city where the German army's advance was halted and then turned back by the heroic Red Army, well, that just doesn't wash . . .

—Why not?

—Simple: because the Russians themselves changed the name of the city. Now it's called Volgograd. Did you know that?

—No, I didn't.

—But you French are more Catholic than the Pope . . .

Jean-Jacques smiled as he rinsed the glasses. He hadn't had a conversation like that for a long time. Not that you can say he missed such conversations. From the very start of their friendship, the barman had realized that Yegor was far from being a man of the left: what he'd experienced in the Soviet Union had probably traumatized him for life. Now, after everything that had happened, after everything he'd found out about the Soviet Union, it was easier for Jean-Jacques to accept an argument with Yegor than it would have been for him years before, when he was an active member of the Communist Party. He'd been a fervent militant who fiercely loved the Party. But many things had changed since then in the world, and in his own mind too. He had shed that blind faith, which had helped him to ignore many things that would otherwise have been hard to understand. But that doesn't mean he'd have been capable, as others had been, of publicly denouncing his past and all his ideas and passions connected to politics or inspired by it. He hadn't even told Yegor about that period of his life. Not that he'd have been embarrassed, but their friendship would have suffered and it would have been a pity . . . Yegor would have asked him whether in his mind communism still represented a goal for mankind, an idea, albeit a utopian one, for which it was worth fighting and even sacrificing yourself. If he'd asked that question, what would he have answered? It wasn't at all easy to answer. And so he preferred not to give his friend the opportunity to ask such questions. Ultimately, the relationship between them, although friendly, wasn't so close, so intimate, that he felt obliged to tell Yegor everything that weighed on his soul. For example, he didn't tell him about the dreams he'd been having ever since the beautiful stranger first appeared in the café.

And it was a good thing that he didn't, because look who was coming through the door: Yegor, accompanied by the beautiful stranger. The man entered first, he held the door wide open and with impeccable politeness he stepped aside for the beautiful woman, who, by her accent and her resemblance to the actress, Elvire Popesco, was almost certainly Romanian.

You might say that she bumped into Yegor outside the bistro, purely by chance . . . But hadn't she seen him from a distance and didn't she deliberately slow her steps? She didn't stop to look in the window of the porcelain shop as she always did otherwise, and she didn't go into the bookshop on the corner of the street which she had to cross so that twenty or thirty meters later she'd arrive in front of Jean-Jacques's bar at the same time as Yegor. You might also say that he'd seen the beautiful stranger, who his friend the barman adamantly claimed was Romanian.

—Why not Russian? he asked, just pretending, so as to annoy him.

But to cut a long story short: it was no accident. Not only did he see her, but also he'd waited by the Métro station, behind a newspaper stand. For almost an hour. His back was aching from waiting so long. But he'd had no choice. The day before, he'd received a telephone call giving him very precise instructions . . .

Maybe he'd tried to breathe the little air that seeped under the door. But had he had the strength to crawl that far? That was the question . . . Or rather, had he had the time to get out of bed, crawl on all fours and put his nose to the crack under the door? Probably he'd died in his sleep. Asphyxiated by the gas from the stove . . . Gassed!

—He didn't suffer . . .

—Apparently you don't suffer. It all happens gradually, the same as under anesthesia when the dose is too high: the heart stops before so-called consciousness starts functioning again. You don't suffer and you're not afraid. It's best that way.

—Are you afraid?

—Yes, I'm afraid. Why are you looking at me like that? What are you trying to do? Scare me? I'm afraid. I'm not ashamed to say it . . . Take your paws off my throat! It hurts! What are you doing?

Yegor chuckled and got out of bed. He looked at the empty vodka bottle on the bedside table.

—Mother was afraid too, Ana went on. She wanted to live. To live whatever the cost, although she knew very well that the battle was one-sided, you can't snatch yourself from the claws of cancer so easily as that. Especially not in the Romania of those days . . .

—It's empty, said Yegor, waving the bottle above his head.

—Yes, it's empty. What do you want me to do about it?

—Don't you have another?

—Why would I have another? I didn't even drink vodka before I met you . . . It was you who taught me to drink this rotgut.

Yegor remembered that in Jean-Jacques's bar, before he met her, the barman had been very excited to tell him that the beautiful stranger, as he called her, had ordered a vodka. But he didn't bother to remind her. What was the point? What good would it have done? The thing was, he ought to have brought two bottles with him. The same as he'd done at the beginning of their relationship. She hadn't been very happy about it. She'd become all haughty and sanctimonious and told him the story of that Romanian poet who had drunk himself to death with vodka.

—He must have been soft, that poet of yours, said Yegor, scornfully.

—His mother was Russian. A Russian princess who fled to Romania just after the revolution . . .

—Is that so? A real princess? Princesses cropped up everywhere after the revolution, like mushrooms after the rain . . .

Fine, then! She didn't want him turning up with two bottles

of vodka? The next day he arrived carrying one bottle instead of two. The other bottle he left in the corner outside the door, and when the first ran out—all things come to an end!—he got out of bed, without even pulling on his long johns, and merely opened the door . . . "You're insane!" shouted Ana. But in the end, when he invited her to drink, she didn't refuse. In fact, she liked to tipple . . . But Yegor quickly realized that he had nothing to gain if he rubbed her nose in her own contradiction. She had contradictions too, thank God . . . Polite, even in his own mind, Yegor termed them contradictions.

—She was afraid, obviously. She screamed her head off in her hospital bed. Not so much from the pain, since they stuffed her with painkillers, and toward the end they also gave her morphine. A doctor took pity on her; usually they only administered morphine at the very end, since they were making economies. Understand?

—Didn't she believe in God?

—In God? Maybe only in the devil . . . Anyway, she was always cursing by the devil . . .

—Didn't the priest come?

—Of course not! You ask as if you hadn't lived in a communist country yourself . . . How could the priest have come to the hospital?

—Yes . . . You're right . . .

Yegor got out of bed again and went to the kitchen to look inside the refrigerator. Even a bottle of wine was better than nothing . . .

After her father's death, she had a recurring dream in which he wasn't dead, but hiding somewhere, in a provincial small town, at the house of some friends his wife never knew he had. A run-down small town in northern Moldavia. "Why northern Moldavia?" said her mother in amazement. Ana shrugged. She didn't bother explaining to her that she heard the people in the dream talking in that well-known Moldavian accent, Elvira in particular . . . Her mother would have asked who Elvira was and Ana didn't want to endure one of her interrogations. Or to hear her making fun of her. Sofica didn't believe in dreams or astrology. One day, when she caught her daughter looking through a work on astrology that she'd bought in a second-hand bookshop, she chided her mockingly, almost furiously.

—It's complete nonsense! For gullible, daydreaming teenage girls!

—You talk like the communists, Ana muttered, without looking up from the yellowed pages of the book.

—God created man in His image and likeness . . .

Thus spoke Johannes, beginning the speech which she, having heard it a number of times, in its different versions, knew quite well. Later, if she made an effort, she could remember it, at least broadly, even if in places she couldn't hit on the right term.

While the ancient gods, the gods of Egypt in particular, started out with the forms of animals, it wasn't until the Greeks that they gradually became anthropomorphized, but in their physical more than their moral or psychic aspects. They were not omnipotent. Each of them had a predominant feature and a field of action where what they said went. The Greek gods were in fact explanations of various natural phenomena, which the people of that time feared without being able to understand them. Each god was responsible for a different phenomenon. They had a kind of boss, or rather a father, who was a lecher and at the same time creator. Zeus . . . Anyway, Greek mythology is more complicated than that, but broadly speaking, the gods were connected with nature. They were nature's representatives in man's mind.

But the monotheistic God is both more abstract and more powerful than Zeus. He was modelled on man himself, but not man as an individual . . . Here was the great innovation!

The genius of it was also that it was the result of a complicated, unconscious process. God isn't the mankind of one or another era. The monotheistic God represents the human species in essence; He contains all the human species' qualities . . .

—Both good and bad? asked Hannah—or Ana, if you prefer—but Johannes didn't answer this question, since he didn't want to get sidetracked from what he had to say.

—Let's not have any pointless parentheses, he decreed and continued his lecture.

This is why what has been happening since Nietzsche, or since Feuerbach and Marx to be more precise, is dangerous. Sick of all that blind faith, man starts out asking questions and ends up negating the God he's accepted hitherto. He kills Him! yelled Johannes. Man kills the God he himself created. That's what's called . . .

—What is it called? shouted Johannes Schneide.

—Patricide . . . whispered Hannah.

—No . . . You haven't understood anything! It's not patricide; it's infanticide. It's the temptation identified even as early as the Old Testament: that of making sure of the present at any price, even at the price of the future. Remember that Abraham was ready to kill his son . . . In other words, to kill the future. At the symbolic level, it means killing the species. If the human species vanishes, the idea of God vanishes along with it. In the Old Testament, the act isn't carried through to the very end. But what about later? Don't you think that the crucifixion of Jesus is along the same lines? It's infanticide . . . Father, why have you abandoned me? The question is tantamount to an accusation. It's poor Isaac all over again, groaning and weeping. But this time, there's no escape. The idea of the death of God starts to take root at the same time as the crucifixion. Although nobody realized it. In any case, not straightaway. Maybe only the Jews, who stubbornly rejected that new religion . . . Resurrection? Did you say resurrection?

—I didn't say it . . . I didn't say anything. *Mea culpa!* said poor Hannah.

—This demagogy about the resurrection is unacceptable. And ultimately ineffectual. For, if that reckless promise helped the spread of Christianity in a naïve and at the same time desperate polytheistic world, its brazen irrationality hastened the loss of faith and ultimately led to atheism. Religion's main defect is its anachronism. After so many centuries of triumphant reason and science, how do you expect man to believe in resurrection anymore? Nietzsche, for example, was influenced not only by Schopenhauer, but also by Darwin. And later by Dostoevsky, an atheist tortured by the idea of death . . .

Fear gripped Hannah: his eyes bulging, Schneide, the German philosopher, had risen from his armchair and was striding around the house, swinging his arms. At one point, he raised his right arm, as if pointing up at the ceiling, but probably our metaphysician's intention was to pass beyond—beyond the ceiling, I mean . . . He suddenly stopped. He turned to Hannah, who was still sitting on her chair, her thighs closely pressed against each other, she felt a great weariness, a feeling of faintness, as if after prolonged bleeding . . .

—Once He has been killed, can you tell me what to put in His place?

Hannah shook her head a number of times. No, she couldn't say. She didn't have the faintest idea . . .

In other words, Johannes went on, man gave up the God he had imagined and patiently constructed for so many centuries, he gave up the God who represented the essence of the human species. And primarily, he gave up all that was good in man and which was worthy of conservation. Besides, it was out of his obsession with conservation that man invented writing. You understand? Which of course is what led to progress, to the perfection of mankind, although not man as an individual. I might even say that the individual is regressing. For example, he has less and less of a need for memory . . . Now that he has invented writing . . . You see? Now that it no longer has any exercise, the memory is weakening. The invention of writing was one of the first capital errors! Plato understood this immediately . . . Anyway, mankind has, let's say, been evolving, particularly when it comes to science, to knowledge of the environment. But what about the individual? The gap between the poor individual and the potential of the species and even its achievements hitherto has become greater and greater. The individual has become infantilized, he's regressing, I might even say that he's becoming a kind of spoiled child. He demands to be coddled—by society, by the community—he constantly craves protection and assistance. He benefits from all the inventions of modern civilization without any understanding of how they've come about, let alone how they function. Faced with so many miraculous gadgets, all he knows how to do is press a button. That's on the one hand, but on the other, along with progress, belief in God starts being put sorely to the test and in the end it can't hold out. How could it hold out? Atheism is infectious!

—Most seriously of all, added Johannes, somewhat more calmly, is that man taken as an individual is placed on a pedestal and tends to replace God, which is to say, he's elevated higher than the essence of the human species. The individual is higher than the species! The rights of the individual are more important than those of the species . . .

When Johannes reached this point in his speech, a key point, we might say, poor Ana lost the thread of the argument. To her, species, the essence of mankind, and all the rest were notions too abstract.

—Why is it so serious to grant importance to the rights of the individual? ventured Hannah. What about the French Revolution? Or even the October Revolution?

The German gave a scornful wave of the hand. "This Johannes is a bit of a reactionary," thought Hannah. "But he fondly thinks he's a man of the left! And an ecologist to boot . . . Maybe he's an out-and-out fascist . . ." Of course, Hannah didn't dare fling the accusation of being a fascist in his face. And so she stood up and tried to change the subject or even to staunch his oratorical surge under one pretext or another. But how can you staunch German speculative thought?

It wasn't of her that Jean-Jacques dreamed, not of Ana, but of Elvire, who in his mind remained as young and beautiful as she'd been in the days when he saw her in the movies. She appeared to him in a room with red wallpaper, playing with a parrot as big as an eagle, to which she talked, to which she muttered sweet nothings, and there in its cage the parrot let out all kind of strange croaks, probably in Romanian. He could see Elvire only from behind, she was wearing a nightdress, and in fact he couldn't be certain it was she, it might very well have been the other woman, whose name was Elena and who had died two or three months previously, shot dead on Christmas Day. Or maybe it was Ana, although when he began to dream of her, which was just a few days before, his dreams had been much more dynamic or, it might even be said, downright violent. She looked like a cadaver in one of those sliding shelves in the morgue. Jean-Jacques pulled the body out of that long box and carried it to a bed. No, she didn't smell of death. That was certain . . . She smelled of flowers. Jean-Jacques sniffed her nipples, as if they were flowers. And her armpits. He ran his tongue over one of her nipples, sucked it, nibbled it. He then moved down toward the mole, which he didn't touch; his tongue came to a stop just before it. It went around the mole. Ana didn't so much as flinch. Jean-Jacques was sleeping without his pajamas on, and in any case without his pajama bottoms. She didn't move. Her immobility excited him intensely. But he controlled himself. He groaned. He stretched out beside the woman as motionless as a corpse and for a long time he too remained stock-still.

It isn't possible to recount a dream. True, there was nobody he could have recounted it to. Heh-heh! How he'd have made fun of him . . .

Sometimes, Dieter was there. At such times Johannes's speech became more moderate; it turned into something more like a conversation. Dieter didn't let himself be intimidated the way Hannah did, he'd have his say, express his opinion, contradict Johannes, although in the main he often agreed with him.

—Ultimately, what are you getting at? Dieter interjected. Am I right in thinking that you deplore the decline of religion? If you put it like that, you're wrong. Religion isn't in decline at all. Quite the contrary . . .

—I'm not deploring the decline of religion, Johannes corrected him, I'm deploring the decline of morality. Even if I for one don't need religion in order to construct my own morality. But the ordinary man, the man on the street, doesn't have sufficient strength of character to do without God. He doesn't have enough faith in his own reason. He feels a need to be commanded, to hear a voice from without, from beyond. A voice that can't be contradicted . . .

—Like Abraham! exclaimed Hannah, who passed as Jewish in the two philosophers' eyes.

—Yes, like Abraham, sneered Johannes. But that Abraham of yours stopped before he went too far. Whereas nowadays, modern man, the spoiled brat of human rights, allows himself to exhaust all the world's natural resources, to pollute the air and water . . .

—I get it, interrupted Dieter, you think that the ecologists are right and that the human species itself is in danger. And religion, according to you, because it has engendered a God in the image and likeness of the species, rather than the individual, is destined to temper the selfishness of the individual, who is tempted to cry: *Après moi le déluge!* On that point I'm in agreement with you! Completely in agreement . . .

—What about Noah . . . mumbled Hannah, without very much conviction.

She now remembered her remark with a certain pride, although at the time she'd dared only to utter it sotto voce, while the two men continued their conversation without paying very much attention to her. Noah saved the human species. If there's a danger, i.e. the flood, then naturally there's also a solution, for example Noah . . .

—Religion isn't a solution, she heard Dieter say. Religion, monotheistic religion in particular . . .

—The Christian religion, said Johannes, in corroboration. The most demagogic religion in the world.

—The Hebraic religion is no better! interrupted Dieter. Except that the demagogic strategy is different: it's based not on openness, not on attracting neophytes from all over the world . . .

—Then it's not demagogic in that case!

— . . . but on the promise of privileged relations with the deity. The Hebraic religion promises an alliance with God . . .

—Like any other religion!

— . . . an exclusivist alliance as a demagogic promise. The Jewish people are the chosen people. Chosen to do what? That's what sent Hitler into a deranged jealous rage.

—The master race against the chosen people! Johannes solemnly intoned. Don't you think you're going a bit over the top with that joke?

And he looked at Hannah, who, however, was looking at the kitchen door. The discussion between the two men had exhausted her. After two or three seconds' silence, Dieter went on:

—Not to mention the latecomer, the Muslim religion. Ridiculous in its demagogy, influenced by Christianity . . . And aggressive, extremely aggressive!

—It was spread by the sword, and now, contested by modern civilization, it defends itself through terrorist attacks. But even so, the Christian religion was and is the most demagogic.

—The Christian religion was the logical result of a process whereby the idea of the deity was anthropomorphized, a process which once begun can't be stopped . . . The deity descends to earth to preach brotherly love, love of one's neighbor, which goes beyond even demagogy. It's an attempt at religious globalization: erasure of the differences between spiritual love. And don't forget that it can be interpreted as a postmodern moment, because it has never shied from revisiting polytheism. It invented the idea of the Holy Trinity and an incalculable number of saints. It's monotheism revised and rectified in a polytheistic spirit. That's why it's had so much success. More so . . . Have you read Jonas?

—Of course!

—Well, that expert in Gnosticism . . .

—Who became one of the first philosophers of ecology. Not by chance . . .

—No he wasn't!

Hannah abandoned the battlefield. The discussion was beyond her. She went into the kitchen and looked in the refrigerator for something to drink. She thought the two ecologists might be able to use a beer. But in the refrigerator there was nothing but tomato juice, a bottle of vodka, and some sausages. Vodka would do! On a tray she placed the bottle of vodka, the tomato juice, and three glasses, and feeling in a better mood she went back into the living room. The eyes of the two philosophers glazed with happiness.

Ana smiled tenderly when she remembered the two Krauts and their endless discussions . . .

Not even she knew why she'd told Johannes she was Jewish. The first night, after the cinema and the restaurant, at his house, between passionate embraces, she'd told him she was from Romania. Without further detail. Mihai was against details.

—You always have to keep up an artistic flow, he said with a laugh. Let your interlocutor fill in the blanks . . . Don't be afraid of pauses. That's what they're for. The same as in poetry!

Mihai wasn't joking, he wasn't joking at all.

And indeed, if she'd remained discreet and mysterious, Johannes wouldn't have assailed her with questions. It wasn't his style. He'd have been satisfied with what she told him. He wasn't curious by nature. But with Dieter it would have been more complicated. Dieter would have liked to pry it out of her. And she probably wouldn't have shied away. But by the time they became intimate, there was no longer any need: she'd already told Johannes a whole host of things, and he, probably questioned by Dieter, had conscientiously informed his friend. The two had been bosom buddies ever since lyceum. Johannes cared enormously about his friend from lyceum and university, even though he had a certain advantage over him. This is always what happens in a friendship: one dominates the other. But it's a phantasmal rather than a real domination. Usually, friendship is based on quite a complicated system of compensations. You allow yourself to be dominated in order to dominate . . . It's a kind of permanent *donnant-donnant*. It's not quite the famous Hegelian master-slave relationship. But even so, something of it remains . . .

The truth is that Ana didn't take much notice of Mihai's advice. She was talkative. It's quite a widespread failing in both sexes. In any case, she liked to tell stories, to make up all kinds of things. She'd had this talent or failing since she was at school. When she came back from holiday she used to enthral her schoolmates with all kinds of made-up stories, although they were not completely so. They were only half made up. That was her technique: she'd base a story on a real event and then embroider it. The real event, which was skillfully chosen, was therefore so lifelike that it projected its lifelikeness on the rest. And this helped her to be believed. When she told a story, she herself believed in it, which is why it was so convincing to the ears of others.

But what about Yegor's ears?

It's very hard to answer this question. In the first place, she didn't hesitate to weave a whole story about her departure from Romania (where she'd been a doctor!), having been invited to attend a colloquium in Germany, where she hadn't applied for political asylum, because she didn't like the life there. She preferred Paris and Parisian life, she'd spoken French since childhood, and her parents had spent years in France, before the war. No, it was before she was born . . .

—But what did your parents do in Paris? insisted Yegor.

—What did they do? They had fun!

Yegor looked at her for a good few seconds. Her answer had blurted out spontaneously, and so if she were lying, it wasn't on this point: she really believed that in Paris there was nothing else to do except have fun. Ultimately, she wasn't the only person who thought that way. That great writer with the inflated reputation, Hemingway, didn't think entirely otherwise . . .

"Fortunately for her, the owner one day decided to send her to Italy, where earnings were more substantial. Together with some other women, Aneta crossed the Adriatic on a motorboat, a Zodiac. The craft sank somewhere off the coast of Puglia. Soaking wet, shivering with cold, Aneta and the other women waited in a forest for the truck to take them to Milan, Rome, or Turin. But instead of a truck, the Carabinieri turned up and took them to a special center in Santa Foca. Funded by the Italian state and run by a priest, Don Cesare Lo Deserto, the center was the salvation of Aneta and the other women in her situation."

The article ended with the romance between the Romanian woman and Achimil, a young Iraqi migrant, who worked under the direct supervision of Don Cesare. Jean-Jacques folded up the newspaper and shoved it under the counter.

—What do you think of this article?

—What do you want me to say? sighed Yegor. Pour me another vodka.

From time to time she went to Edouard's studio, where she posed stark naked. The painting was almost finished. She looked at it carefully and puckered her lips. In the painting her breasts looked larger than they really were. She told the painter so, and he laughed.

—In Romania, do all women have such . . . such whopping big breasts?

And he laughed once more. Which is to say, he let out an abrupt whinny. Edouard himself wasn't one hundred per cent French. His father, a ship's captain during the war in Indochina, had been sent home wounded, but accompanied by a beautiful Vietnamese woman, who, after they amputated the captain's left leg, soon became his wife. The beautiful Ho gave birth to Edouard just a few months after the amputation. After Ho returned from the clinic cradling Edouard, the sailor was forced to go back to the military hospital, where they amputated his right leg.

—Next time, you'll wear the blouse, said the painter.

—The *ie*?

—Yes, the Romanian blouse.

—And what about my bottom half?

—No need . . . I'm only interested in your top half. I'm curious as to whether it's too small. Come on, try it on now!

—You don't have any patience . . .

—I just want to see how it fits.

—So, you really want to paint me in this blouse. After Matisse, don't you think it's a risk?

—Why would it be a risk? What could happen to me?

—Nothing, but they'll say you copied him.

—They'll say! And they'll unyoke the oxen from my bicycle! Let them say it . . . Don't you know that the subject doesn't count? My style and my manner of painting are completely different. I'm realistic, much more realistic than Matisse, hyper-realistic, even . . . With a dash of expressionism . . .

Ana shrugged.

Nevertheless, she put on the blouse and went to stand in front of the mirror. She wrinkled her nose, puckered her lips, frowned.

—I don't like it, and that's that. The one Matisse painted wasn't like this . . . And anyway, I need to put a skirt on.

—What do I care what the one Matisse painted was like! said Edouard, losing his temper. I want to paint the blouse I bought specially. And it suits you very well. I've got nothing against it if you want to put a skirt on. Buy a skirt . . . I'll pay for it. It can be a blue one.

—Blue?

—Yes, blue. Didn't you say you wanted it to be like in the Matisse painting? Well, in the Matisse painting, the skirt is blue. And the blouse is white, embroidered with red thread. The same as the French flag, or even the American one . . . Satisfied?

—I'm the one who has to be satisfied?

—How about I paint you wrapped in the American flag?

—I don't want any of that . . . I'm tired and I want to leave; I want to go home to bed.

—All right, it's enough for today. Next time we'll do a few trials. To hit on the most suitable color. But I don't think I'll need you to be here for that; I can do it on the computer . . .

—On the computer?

—Yes, don't be so amazed . . . The computer is a great help to painters. If only Matisse had had a computer!

—I don't understand . . . Matisse with a computer would have been better than the Matisse of sixty, seventy years ago? In his most creative period, I mean.

Edouard didn't say anything for a few seconds: what a sharp tongue the girl had, and she wasn't at all stupid! Ana thought it hadn't been for nothing that she'd cohabited with two German philosophers for months. And she smiled. But not straightaway . . . Edouard hadn't thrown in the towel, however. He went back on the attack.

—All right, let's say that the computer wouldn't have changed Matisse's painting. Although we can't be absolutely certain! But this isn't the right way to think about it. The computer couldn't have come into existence at that time . . . that's what needs to be said. There's a certain concordance between art and science, the same as there is between all the fields of human endeavor. If painting is approaching its end . . .

—Is it approaching or has it gotten there already?

—Gotten where?

Edouard asked the question with such alarm that it sounded downright comical.

—You yourself say it from time to time. And you throw away your paintbrushes and hide your easel behind the cupboard and want to make love all the time. Right now you're going through a more positive, more optimistic phase. You haven't slept with me for almost a month . . .

—A month?

—Yes, approximately a month.

—I see you keep a tally, said Edouard, with a certain amount of satisfaction.

—I keep a tally, of course I do, given that you're less miserly when you make love. Or maybe when you're painting you don't have time to think of anything else, you're focused on your work . . . You can't think of anything else. Least of all money!

It was hard to tell whether the beautiful Romanian, cavorting half naked and wearing nothing but an *ie*, was talking seriously or whether she was just teasing the poor postmodern painter. Edouard looked at her pensively. He'd have liked to go up to her and to place his hand on her hips, her buttocks, to caress her thighs, and then slowly to take off her *ie*, to move his face, his mouth toward her breasts, to kiss them, to suck them, to tweak the nipples between his lips, and then to push her onto the bed . . . But he made no movement, he uttered no word. He seemed frozen rigid. He merely watched as she looked for her panties, her skirt, she took off the *ie*, put on her bra, and then her t-shirt, which clung so tightly to her ample bosoms.

It isn't known why she liked to travel below ground, on the underground railway . . . Like a worm, in fact no, like a mole, as Dieter used to say, making fun of her, since in Berlin too the U-Bahn was her favorite means of locomotion. But now she was in Paris, outside the Réaumur-Sébastopol Métro station. She started to descend the steps. At the bottom, she came across a crouching gypsy woman, who said to her:

—*Hai, frumoaso, mînca-ți-aș ochii, hai să-ți ghicesc viitorul.*

She was struck by the fact that the gypsy woman had addressed her in Romanian. That she knew Romanian wasn't unusual; a lot of gypsies come from Romania or have stayed there for a period and learned the language. Gypsies are polyglots. But how did the gypsy woman know that she spoke the language? She sensed it, divined it . . . Good for her! And so she stopped. She held out her hand. The palm reader took it, looked at it for a few seconds, turned it palm up, palm down, and then palm up again. She was concentrating so hard that her hand trembled. She raised her head to look at Ana, bit her lips, and whispered, still in Romanian:

—May God preserve you!

—Yes, yes, and what else?

—Nothing else. Go, go from here . . .

When she reached the track, the first race had already run. What did it matter! She didn't go to the races to wager, although sometimes she found herself going to a booth to lay a bet and sometimes she even won, small sums, since she didn't gamble large amounts, but even a small win gave her pleasure.

—Might you lend me your binoculars for just a moment, please? I think *La belle Américaine* is out in front, isn't she?

The man with the binoculars turned his head, looked her up and down, and didn't reply. He went on watching the race, through his binoculars. *La belle Américaine* was indeed galloping out in front, but that was no reason for him to relinquish that wonderful instrument, which gave you a close-up view of that furious cavalcade: Bœuf was jerking up and down on the mare's back like a devil, lashing his whip left and right, but the race was far from won. He'd broken away from the rest of the pack too soon; usually, a horse can't hold out in a leading position and will flag before it reaches the finishing line. Ana was left open-mouthed. It wasn't very often that she was treated with such contempt, and so she simply didn't know what to do. On her other side, two young men were jumping up and down and shouting the names of jockeys, including the famous Dominique Bœuf, on whom Ana often wagered, although she knew that no matter how good he might be, he still couldn't win race after race. In the last race he'd come in second, losing by a nose. Bœuf's advantage was that he always inspired hope in the punters who bet on him, he was always among the frontrunners in the battle for victory. A debatable tactic according to some, who reckoned that he should save his energy, remain at the back of the pack and then, at the right moment, usually when they entered the final straight, mount a decisive attack that would bring victory right on the finishing line. But that was what you might call the ideal race! In fact, as a young trainer with whom Ana had gone to a hôtel a few times explained, it all depends on the horse; not all horses are the same, and the jockey needs to pay attention to the trainer's advice. *La belle Américaine* didn't win the race. She crossed the line completely exhausted.

Two or three weeks later, the trainer was to have the uninspired idea of running her in a hurdle race, just as an experiment. *La belle Américaine*, who was built for speed and probably hadn't had enough practice in that kind of race, stumbled and broke a leg. In such cases, a racehorse's career is finished permanently. A veterinarian will arrive to give his opinion, and then the mare will be taken around the back of the racetrack and put down.

A lot of the time, Ana didn't even watch the race. She'd sit on the terrace of the restaurant with a martini or just a coffee. Spring was already turning to summer. Perhaps too quickly . . . The beautiful woman's gaze was absent; she looked melancholy. On the terrace there were also a few other people, who preferred to sit there in peace, sipping fruit juices or alcoholic but nonetheless refreshing beverages, through a straw or straight from the glass, rather than clambering onto the stands, where you couldn't even sit down, since most of the spectators stood up as soon as the race started: they'd stand up one after the other, and those who were determined to remain seated wouldn't be able to see anything of the race, and so they would have to stand up too, climbing on top of the wooden benches, which got dirtier and dirtier, so much so that in the end nobody felt like sitting down. On the terrace there were television screens, on which you could follow the race very well. Better than from the stands. The passionate reader of *Paris-Turf* from Jean-Jacques's bistro was there too. Rather than watching the race, he was absorbed in his interminable calculations. An elegantly dressed, ageing lady, presumably excited by what she could see on the television screen, had stood up and was waving her arms in satisfaction, unconcerned about other people's stares. A very short man, probably a former jockey, was walking among the tables and offering to tell whoever was prepared to listen the name of the horse that would win the next race. Of course, in exchange for this tip, the lucky winner would pay ten per cent of his winnings to the short man. Ana quite quickly understood the nature of the trick. The former jockey proposed a different horse to each person, one of which was bound to win. But since the track habitués knew him to be a sly rogue, he was obliged to seek out if not greenhorns, then at least people who didn't know him. What's for sure is that the short man possessed an exceptional visual memory: rarely did he approach for a second time punters who had followed his tip, betted and lost. Ana saw him approach a blond, rather chubby young man, who, perhaps from timidity, was unable to avoid being drawn into a conversation with him. The former jockey sat down at the table and pointed with a pencil at the winning horse on the program. Ana took a closer look and recognized Ed, who served as a waiter at peak hours in Jean-Jacques's bistro. Her first instinct was to get up, call out to him, or at least give him a sign, so that he wouldn't fall prey to the short man. But then she thought that it was an experience through which he had to pass and that he'd suffer no great loss. And so she remained seated, sipping her martini through a straw. A few minutes later, Ed got up from his table and walked purposefully to the nearest betting booth. The short man had already moved to another table, where he met with less success. The third race was about to run. Ana walked over to the paddock to look at the horses and the jockeys, who were receiving their trainers' final instructions. She saw a handsome gray horse, skittish and apt for great deeds. It had a German name: *Erlkönig*. Moreover, it wore number five, her favorite number. She didn't have to stop to think; she went straight to a betting booth. She laid a hefty bet. And then she walked around a little, looking left and right at the men, almost all of whom had pairs of binoculars hanging around their necks. She didn't see the boorish oaf who had insulted her by refusing, without a word, to lend her his binoculars for a few seconds. In fact, she wouldn't even have recognized him. It wasn't the first time that hatred or annoyance at someone had erased his face from her memory. This was why she didn't hold grudges. She quite simply forgot. How then could she avenge herself on somebody, if she no longer knew who . . . In the present case, she seemed completely to have forgotten the oaf's face, or else she couldn't see him anywhere. What if she'd seen him and recognized him? What would she have done? Maybe he'd been an Englishman who hadn't understood a word she said. But even so, he could have told her in English that he didn't understand, rather than giving her a scornful look. She shrugged and went back to the roof restaurant. Ed was sitting at a table some way away, watching the pre-race preparations. It was taking quite a lot of time for them to push the horses into those stalls that would fly open when the race began. The gray, almost white, horse was cutting all kinds of capers and refused to line up inside the stall. Finally, the race began. Ed was holding a thick wad of betting slips. "The madman has betted his tip money for a whole week," thought Ana and watched as he rose to his feet, which was completely pointless there on the terrace. *Erlkönig* had got off to a slow start and was at the back of the pack. The advantage of a light-colored horse is that it stands out from the others, which all look more or less the same. Ana had the satisfaction of seeing her horse gradually overtake its opponents and reach second or third place. On the final bend it lost a little ground, but gained an advantageous position to the stands side of the still quite compact pack. An ebony-black horse had taken the lead and was heading like a whirlwind for the finishing line. Ed was delirious with excitement. He'd climbed on top of his chair. *Erlkönig* was closing, menacingly. The black horse was called *Beginning of the End*. It was obvious that Ed had betted on it. The short man suddenly made his appearance and tiptoed up to Ed's table. The white and the black horse were now neck and neck. On the horses' backs the jockeys were bouncing up and down like crazed monkeys, frantically lashing with their whips, shouting, cursing, threatening. The finishing line was now in sight and nobody could have said for sure which of the two horses was going to win. It would be a photo finish. Ed climbed down off his chair and stooped to hug the short man. He then turned and saw Ana, he recognized her and went up to her, waving his betting slips. The short man tailed him at a distance.

—Bravo! said Ana. Did you bet on *Erlkönig*?

—No. I bet on *Beginning of the End* . . . It won!

—Not so fast, we don't know yet, said Ana, trying to dampen his enthusiasm, but the small waiter, who had never been to the races before, didn't have the slightest doubt. He turned to the short man, as if calling on him as a witness. The short man nodded encouragingly.

—You're in for a whopping win, said the former jockey.

—Did you lay a large bet? Ana asked without embarrassment.

The short man pricked up his ears. But Ed was too much of a greenhorn to try to bamboozle him. He had indeed laid a hefty bet, and announced the sum without a moment's hesitation.

—I bet on *Erlkönig*, said Ana. But only twenty euros. It would be better if you won, Ed. Ed was unsurprised that the beautiful Romanian woman had suddenly started addressing him informally, by his first name. He was happy . . .

He ordered drinks for all three. Ana opted for another martini. Ed and the short man drank beer. After they'd clinked glasses like old friends, they heard the announcement that *Beginning of the End* was the winner. The short man was now more enthusiastic than Ed. He realized that he was in for a hefty sum. He'd found the ideal mark.

—They'll start paying out in a few minutes, he said. You ought to join the line. Would you like me to keep your place for you?

—Good idea! said Ed and starting counting the winning slips.

—My name is actually Edmond.

—Is it? Pleased to meet you . . . It's a very nice name, said Ana and got out of bed to go to the bathroom.

Meanwhile, Edmond wondered whether she was being ironic or not . . . And whether he'd lived up to the standards of that magnificent woman. Through the window could be seen the Eiffel Tower.

—It's like the name of a character in a novel, added Ana, when she came back, her breasts jiggling perkily.

My Dear Mihai,

I waited for you in Berlin almost nine months and you didn't come, unlike you promised. I know that it's not easy for you, especially after everything that has happened and has been happening lately. And that you couldn't have guessed that what happened was going to happen. Although when you left Berlin, maybe you hinted at it. There are hard times ahead, you told me. I asked you why. But know I understand what you meant. Maybe you said it because you knew about what was in store. You were in on the secret of the gods. In which case maybe it will be better for you. And if it's better for you, won't it be better for me too? But maybe you knew about it only by chance, in which case I don't know what to say. This is why I beg you from the bottom of my heart to write me a few lines, to enlighten me.

I'm well, in good health, but very depressed. Depressed and uneasy. Not only because I haven't had any news from you. I don't know how to explain it. I'm tortured by all kinds of evil premonitions. I have bad dreams, real nightmares. I feel like I'm being followed, in danger. I met a man who seemed nice at first. He's originally from Russia, but I don't think it's his origins that make me suspect him, because he was Russian even in the beginning, when I first met him. He's a heavy drinker. Obviously, there are plenty of other men who are too, that's not what bothers me, but I get the impression that he's pretending to be more of an alcoholic than he really is. Do you know what I mean? I'm very familiar with pretending. Didn't you used to tell me that I was the queen of the simulacrum? And if he's only pretending to be an alcoholic . . . But at the same time he also plays the part of the jealous man. It's obviously all an act! A jealous, alcoholic Russian, straight out of a novel by Dostoevsky . . .

The other day, in the Métro, I was sitting reading a magazine. The man opposite me, I think he was an Arab, touched my knee with his fingers. At first, I didn't take any notice, I thought to myself that he hadn't done it deliberately, these things happen. A few seconds later, he touched me again, with the palm of his hand, this time harder. I looked at him and asked him what he wanted. He can't have been more than thirty. Maybe younger. He was nasty looking, with a shaved head, badly dressed.

—I think I know you from somewhere, he said.

It was all right; he was just trying to pick me up. I gave him a sour smile and went on reading.

—I'm not joking, he said, aren't you from Romania?

I pricked up my ears, but I controlled myself and said nothing.

—I have to get off now, he went on, but I'll call you on the phone so that we can talk some more. That's because I like you.

He then moved closer and whispered in my ear:

—Keep your eyes peeled. Somebody has it in for you . . .

And then he vanished.

I didn't understand any of it. What was it to him if I come from Romania! Had somebody sent him? Somebody from Romania? For an instant I thought that you had sent him. But why then didn't he tell me straight out that it was on your behalf? And he didn't give the code word. The thing is, I'd like to go back to our country, even if I can imagine that it won't be easy there now for somebody like me . . . I'd like to go back and to be with you again. Close to you, even if you're living with another woman. I'm afraid! Harassment on the Métro is an everyday occurrence here. Almost all the newspapers write about it. Gangs of young men from the Paris suburbs attack you in broad daylight and nobody dares to intervene.

But I'm also afraid when I stay at home. I don't know, maybe I'm wrong, I'd like to be mistaken . . . but believe me, I'm not exaggerating at all. I don't know who it was who said that life is a dream. What can I say . . . If it be so, then a nightmare would be a better way of putting it. That's what my life is: a nightmare. I'm in a state of unbearable waiting. And I don't know what it is I'm waiting for . . .

Anyway, I await a letter from you. Please be kind to me! Remember the time when we were together in Dresden, and then

Prague. I can't write more, because I can feel my tears welling up. Mihai, I still love you.

Ana

—Lost at the races again? Jean-Jacques asked the inveterate reader of *Paris-Turf,* who, having ordered a coffee, had buried his nose in his paper. He was making all kinds of cabbalistic pencil marks on the newspaper, after which he'd look in a notebook, or rather an almanac, which listed almost every active racehorse: next to each horse he wrote down its latest results and other useful observations. For him, betting on the horses wasn't just another pastime, but a scientific endeavor, something unintelligible to all but those very few who fell into the same category as he. In any case, it was unintelligible to Jean-Jacques. Nevertheless, he stood there waiting for an answer. Merely out of the politeness incumbent upon a café proprietor. Perhaps he'd previously asked the same question, and the entire scene had played out before, exactly the same or with variations, as often happens in life. But the racing man didn't deign to reply or to look up from his interminable calculations. Jean-Jacques gave up waiting for a reply and went back to the bar. In the corner, Ed was grinning.

She carefully pulled on the *ie*, lest it tear; it was made of a very sheer material, raw silk. She sat down on the chair, waiting for the painter to approach his easel and continue the portrait he'd been working on for more than two months. With interruptions, obviously. She was unable to pose for more than two hours a week. In vain did Edouard assail her with telephone calls. Once, Yegor had answered. That evening, the Russian had left shouting: "A whore, that's what you are, nothing but a whore!"

Instead of getting down to work, Edouard left the studio, muttering something. All she was able to catch was that he'd be back and that she should stay there, dressed up in that fancy blouse, which he'd procured who knows where. She said nothing. She sat motionless. The sound of the door slamming shut caused her to start. She closed her eyes. Just a quarter of an hour later, Edouard came back carrying a plastic bag, from which he took a packet of coffee, a bag of sugar, and a box of bonbons. Ana made no reaction; she went on sitting, with her head bowed.

—Why so sad? asked the painter.

Ana didn't answer straightaway. She shrugged. She felt her tears welling up. Edouard went over to her and laid his hand on the top of her head. She burst into tears.

—I'm sick of it . . . I'm sick of the life I lead. I can't go on! I want to go back . . . I want to go home!

Edouard stroked her head without saying a word.

—So, you were in the RER. On what line?

—I don't know the line . . . I was going to Denfert-Rocheteau.

—*Rochereau.* So, the RER, B line . . . Edgar, shut that damned door, there's a draught. To continue . . . How many of them were there?

—Three. An Arab and two blacks. Except that one of the blacks wasn't very black . . .

—How do you know he was an Arab? All right, let's skip that. They spoke French, obviously . . .

—Better than I do, said Ana, and looked the policeman straight in the eye. He'd raised his eyes and his hands from the computer keyboard and was looking at her admiringly. It wasn't every day that you saw such a beautiful woman!

—Don't say that . . . You speak French very well! Where are you from?

—Romania. My parents lived in Paris before the war.

—Very nice. Please continue.

—But I was born in Romania, I went to school there . . .

—Yes, very good. Tell me what else happened!

—Well, all three sat down on the seat opposite me and started making fun of me. They were making all kinds of lewd remarks and gestures. I was reading a book. I wasn't looking at them . . .

—What book?

—*Pigeon Post.*

—Excellent. Continue . . .

—And so I was paying attention to the book, rather than to them. Maybe that was what annoyed them, that I was ignoring them. After a while, one of them snatched my handbag and started rummaging in it. I didn't have any great sum of money, but I had all my documents, in particular my passport . . .

—In what name?

—My name: Hannah Silbermann.

—Continue!

—I went on reading. One of them said: "Look where she lives, in the sixteenth. Hannah Sil-ber-mann. She's a Yid, brothers! One hundred per cent . . ."

—And are you?

—No, only my mother's husband, who wasn't really my father, which is to say, he was, because I have his surname, but he was my stepfather . . .

—What was your father called?

—I don't know. My mother didn't tell me.

—What did they call you at school?

—At school? Silbermann.

—Very well, look, I'll give you a piece of paper and you'll write out a declaration that you have lost your passport . . .

—But I didn't lose it; it was stolen.

—Write what I say. I the undersigned . . . the name you said.

—Hannah.

—How do you spell it? With an H?

—Yes, with an H and two N's, but you can write it without an H too. In Romania, people call me Ana . . . The same as the French Anne. It's a name found in every language.

—Yes, fine, write it down.

—Shall I also write that they drew three swastikas on my belly?

—They did that to you?

—Yes. I was wearing one of those short blouses. I didn't want to come here dressed like that. But that was what I was wearing in the Métro. They drew three swastikas on me, with a felt-tip pen. Around my belly button. The Arab did it. He also drew one on my chest, here, by my throat, but I rubbed it off, so I wouldn't be seen like that.

—Swastikas, you say?

—Yes, swastikas. I can show them to you if you like. I didn't rub them off, I didn't even wash my belly, so that I could show them if required. They also wanted to draw a hammer and sickle on me. "She's a Yid from Romania," they said. "A communist!"

—Then things are getting serious, very serious, even . . . Edgar! Come here!

Edgar was tall and looked very young. He had a shock of red hair. His movements were lithe, nonchalant, even. He spoke in a drawl.

—What's up?

—The lady was attacked in the Métro by three anti-Semites.

—You don't say! That's serious!

—I do say. She has three swastikas on her belly . . . Pull your blouse up a little. You have a very nice blouse.

—It's an *ie*. A Romanian blouse, said Ana and took it off in a single motion, revealing her breasts and belly button, above which were drawn three clumsy swastikas.

Probably the Arab or Negro who had drawn them had been distracted by the sight of her breasts. So thought the two policemen, whose faces were bright red, perspiring.

—We need to report this to the chief, said the policeman at the computer and stood up, not knowing what to do with himself, so flustered was he. Beatrice, his wife, had handsome breasts, but they had nothing on these . . .

—He's not here yet, said the other policeman, the ginger one.

—No matter. We'll wait.

—I don't have time to wait, protested Ana and put back on the *ie*.

—You have to get to work?

—Yes . . .

—No problem. We'll give you a note. Where do you work?

—At the Romanian embassy.

—In what position?

—I'm not allowed to say.

—Very well. But please write out a declaration and give us a description of the perpetrators.

—I've just told you . . .

—In greater detail. Edgar will write it down. He'll even make a sketch of their features. He's talented at drawing. He can do your portrait as quick as you can blink.

—I can't give you details, because I didn't get a good look at them . . .

—How so?

—As I told you, I was reading. And then they held my head down while they rummaged in my bag. One of them put his hand on the back of my neck and pressed down on it. I was forced to sit like that for minutes on end. It was terrible!

—What about the swastikas?

—What about them?

—Didn't you get a look at your attackers when they drew the swastikas?

—A black man covered my eyes with the palm of his hand. All I could see was his palm, which was pink . . . and smelled of oranges . . .

—Of what?

—Of tangerines . . .

—And didn't you struggle?

—What would've been the point? It would have turned out even worse. One of them pulled out a shish. I couldn't see his face, just the shish.

—And nobody intervened. Nobody came to your defense?

—Nobody. There weren't many people in the carriage. Two or three elderly people. A woman with a child. It all happened quite quickly. The Arabs got off at the next station. Maybe the other passengers didn't even see what was going on at the other end of the carriage.

—They didn't see? The policeman ceased tapping at the computer keyboard. It means you don't have any witnesses . . .

—I don't know . . . I don't think so . . .

—Yes, well. Write out the declaration that you have lost your documents and then sign it.

—You turn your life into a novel, said Dieter out of the blue.

His face was covered in shaving foam; in his right hand he held a razor and in his left a towel. He'd come out of the bathroom, because he'd run out of patience, he simply had to tell her the sentence or rather the quotation that had been struggling deep in his memory, trying to emerge into the light.

—What do you mean?

—Nothing serious. I mean that your imagination plays a huge part in your life story. It probably makes it more passionate, more meaningful. In any event, more expressive . . . "Life must not be a novel that is given to us," said Novalis. Have you heard of Novalis?

—Vaguely, muttered Hannah.

— . . . but a novel that is made by us."

Barely had she fallen asleep—it was late, past midnight—when she thought she heard a door creaking. The front door of the apartment? Yegor didn't have a key. Nor did Mihai have a key, for the simple reason that they hadn't seen each other since she arrived in Paris. The last time they'd spoken over the telephone had been when she was still in Berlin, not in Kreuzberg, no, she'd left there by then: it had been when she was living now at Johannes's, now at Dieter's. In fact, it had been she who had telephoned him. They'd only spoken for a few minutes. "Where are you?" she screamed. He didn't tell her.

There was definitely somebody on the other side of her bedroom door. For a few days she'd been locking it. She pulled the covers up to her chin and would have pulled them over her head, but they were not long enough and she didn't want her feet to poke out the other end. Ever since she was little she'd hated sleeping with her feet uncovered.

—Are you afraid somebody might tug your feet? her father would joke.

—Who would do that?

—The Old Crone of the Forest . . .

If only she'd brought the birdcage with the eagle into the room . . . If only she'd put it on the bed! An eagle is a daunting sight, more daunting than, say, a parrot. She thought of getting out of bed and fetching the eagle from the closet, but she didn't dare. Her hand groped for the mobile telephone she always left on the bedside table when she went to bed. She should call the police! From the other side of the door, she heard a man's voice, she thought it was Yegor's, but she couldn't be sure:

—Open up! Open up!

There seemed to be two men. Both of them were panting with the effort and excitement. They were hammering at the door with their fists, and then banging it with their shoulders. She was trembling under the blanket, her teeth were chattering, she kept stammering: "I won't open it, I won't . . ." And the door opened, torn off its hinges, Yegor and Jean-Jacques burst into the room, she kept her eyes closed, but still she could see them, then she could feel them, in bed next to her, on top of her, their hands brutally tearing off her pajamas, rending them. One of the two men held her spread-eagled and tried to kiss her, the other pulled down her pajama bottoms, and because she was struggling, he was unable to insert his enormous, bloodied member between her legs. She was screaming at the top of her lungs, and so they held a pillow over her mouth, her groans were now muffled, the man's member had penetrated her, and she felt a wave of warmth wash over her.

She awoke soaked in sweat and sat up in bed. Day was breaking. She got up and dragged herself to the bathroom. She sat down in the bathtub and turned on both taps. The water was too hot. She stretched out her arm and turned off the hot tap. She felt good in the water. Water soothes both the soul and physical pain. It isn't for nothing that people who cut their veins do so while sitting in water, warm water that gradually turns red with blood, as life slowly ebbs away; if you have taken a few sleeping pills beforehand, you fall asleep and maybe you dream. It's no big thing to commit suicide . . .

—Hello? Who's calling?

—It's me . . . Mihai . . .

—Mihai? Your voice is different . . .

—You're mistaken.

—Hello? Is that you, Mihai?

—It's me . . .

—It's a very bad line. Speak louder! What did you say? What did you say I had to do?

—Nothing. You have to wait.

—Mihai, come to me! I'm afraid! Hello, Mihai! What do I have to wait for? For whom? Hello? Hello?

—There's no point in discussing death . . . Death doesn't resemble anything. Any analogy is hazardous. We can't imagine it, the same as we can't imagine God. And then we're tempted to say that He doesn't exist. It's the same with death . . .

—You can't say death doesn't exist. Everybody has seen a dead person.

—If I see a dead person, it doesn't mean I can imagine how he died. What happened when . . . It's the same with God . . .

—How so? You can't mean to say that . . .

—Yes, I think it is. What we call God is that infinite hole through which we vanish forever, the giant magnet that tugs us into non-being.

She'd felt good in Germany. She almost felt like saying she'd been happy. Both among the Turks of Kreuzberg and in the arms of the two philosophy teachers, with whom she'd been part of a beautiful *ménage à trois* at one point. They weren't by any means great in bed, but they were very bright, they knew a whole host of things, she liked them, or in any event she wasn't embarrassed to talk in front of them, and she listened to them and more often than not understood what they were talking about. That gave her as much pleasure as the sex. Maybe even more so, because she wasn't used to it . . .

She climbed into the first vacant taxi she found on the lane. Shortly before she'd spotted Yegor, who was probably spying on her, as usual. She was sick to the back teeth of him! A few days previously she'd seen him in Longchamp, at the racetrack. It was obvious he wasn't interested in the races. He'd followed her there . . .

She opened the door to her apartment and found Edith there. She hadn't finished the cleaning yet. And how could she have finished if she was sitting on the edge of the bed enthralled, listening to the passionate sounds, or rather the groans, issuing from the small tape recorder? Ana had left it under the bed again!

—What are you doing, Edith? What are you listening to?

Edith tittered, not at all embarrassed.

—It's amusing, she said. I'm going to buy myself one. But where did you get one so small . . . I haven't seen one so small except in James Bond movies!

Then she looked at Ana, who couldn't be bothered to talk about it. The eagle's cage was on the windowsill, so that the poor bird could enjoy a little sunshine. It spread its wings, as yet unable to fill the whole space of its prison. But it wouldn't be long before it did . . .

—It doesn't have any room. It's grown so fast!

—I'll be finished before long, said Edith.

—Give it back, now, said Ana, raising her voice, and retrieved the device.

She went into the next room to get a book from the bookcase. But she didn't have the patience to read it. From the next room came the noise of the vacuum cleaner. At last, Edith had decided to finish the cleaning. She was vacuuming busily.

Whenever Yegor said he was coming round, Ana put the eagle's cage in the closet and locked it. The eagle would look at her bitterly, reproachfully, it would shake its feathers, puff them up, and then resign itself, huddle up limply, like a rain-drenched turkey. This time, Ana didn't put the birdcage in the closet; she even left it open. The eagle didn't take advantage straightaway. If it left the cage, where would it go? Ana thought to open the window, but postponed such a decision. Edith had left. Ana was waiting, but she didn't know for what exactly. For Yegor to come? True, she'd just seen him in the Bois de Boulogne, but maybe he was sick of acting the part of the jealous lover. For the last few days, he'd kept asking her to give him a key to the apartment.

—I've only got one, she'd said, and I'm not allowed to make a copy.

Yegor stared at her and exclaimed, almost with admiration:

—You've really got some nerve!

In any event, she was adamant; she wasn't going to open the door to him. Let him break it down. If he tried, she'd call the police. She'd call the station where she had been a few days previously. The two policemen in front of whom she'd taken off her blouse, to show them the swastikas around her belly button, which she herself had . . . anyway, the two policemen would be only too happy to come to her assistance.

She went into the bathroom, but didn't turn on the taps. She undressed without haste, like a professional stripper, and admired herself at leisure in the mirror. After which she burst into tears. She sat down on the bidet. She didn't want to look in the mirror ever again! She stared into space. She sat like that for a long while. Finally she stood up and turned on first one tap and then the other. It was right then that somebody started knocking on the front door. Maybe she heard it, but she didn't budge. It grew louder. The knocking was now a thumping. Somebody was pounding the door with his fist. Ana stood up. She saw a nail file on the glass shelf above the sink: a big one, almost as big as a carpenter's rasp. She grabbed it and with taut lips, knitted brows, she went to the door. She was holding the nail file in her clenched fist, brandishing it at the door like a weapon. The person outside was now punching and kicking the door, which was made of solid wood. Ana stood naked in front of the door. She leaned against the door sash. "Who's there?" No answer.

—Is that you, Yegor?

The door quaked beneath the blows from the other side. Don't open it . . . Don't open it . . . She took two steps back. But what if it was Mihai?

—Is that you, Mihai? Have you come? Have you come at last, my love? I'll open the door for you, yes, I'll open it.

She turned the key twice in the lock and yanked the door handle . . .

DUMITRU TSEPENEAG is one of the most innovative Romanian writers of the second half of the twentieth century. In 1975, while he was in France, his citizenship was revoked by Ceaucescu, and he was forced into exile. In the 1980s, he started to write in French. He returned to his native language after the Ceaucescu regime ended, but continues to write in his adopted language as well.

A native of Sunderland, England, ALISTAIR IAN BLYTH has resided for many years in Bucharest. His many translations from Romanian include: *Little Fingers* by Filip Florian; *Our Circus Presents* by Lucian Dan Teodorovici (available from Dalkey Archive Press); *Occurrence in the Immediate Unreality* by Max Blecher; and *Coming from an Off-Key Time* by Bogdan Suceava.

MICHAL AJVAZ, *The Golden Age.*
The Other City.

PIERRE ALBERT-BIROT, *Grabinoulor.*

YUZ ALESHKOVSKY, *Kangaroo.*

FELIPE ALFAU, *Chromos.*
Locos.

JOE AMATO, *Samuel Taylor's Last Night.*

IVAN ÂNGELO, *The Celebration.*
The Tower of Glass.

ANTÓNIO LOBO ANTUNES, *Knowledge of Hell.*
The Splendor of Portugal.

ALAIN ARIAS-MISSON, *Theatre of Incest.*

JOHN ASHBERY & JAMES SCHUYLER, *A Nest of Ninnies.*

ROBERT ASHLEY, *Perfect Lives.*

GABRIELA AVIGUR-ROTEM, *Heatwave and Crazy Birds.*

DJUNA BARNES, *Ladies Almanack.*
Ryder.

JOHN BARTH, *Letters.*
Sabbatical.

DONALD BARTHELME, *The King.*
Paradise.

SVETISLAV BASARA, *Chinese Letter.*

MIQUEL BAUÇÀ, *The Siege in the Room.*

RENÉ BELLETTO, *Dying.*

MAREK BIENCZYK, *Transparency.*

ANDREI BITOV, *Pushkin House.*

ANDREJ BLATNIK, *You Do Understand.*
Law of Desire.

LOUIS PAUL BOON, *Chapel Road.*
My Little War.
Summer in Termuren.

ROGER BOYLAN, *Killoyle.*

IGNÁCIO DE LOYOLA BRANDÃO, *Anonymous Celebrity.*
Zero.

BONNIE BREMSER, *Troia: Mexican Memoirs.*

CHRISTINE BROOKE-ROSE, *Amalgamemnon.*

BRIGID BROPHY, *In Transit.*
The Prancing Novelist.

GERALD L. BRUNS, *Modern Poetry and the Idea of Language.*

GABRIELLE BURTON, *Heartbreak Hotel.*

MICHEL BUTOR, *Degrees.*
Mobile.

G. CABRERA INFANTE, *Infante's Inferno.*
Three Trapped Tigers.

JULIETA CAMPOS, *The Fear of Losing Eurydice.*

ANNE CARSON, *Eros the Bittersweet.*

ORLY CASTEL-BLOOM, *Dolly City.*

LOUIS-FERDINAND CÉLINE, *North.*
Conversations with Professor Y.
London Bridge.

MARIE CHAIX, *The Laurels of Lake Constance.*

HUGO CHARTERIS, *The Tide Is Right.*

ERIC CHEVILLARD, *Demolishing Nisard.*
The Author and Me.

MARC CHOLODENKO, *Mordechai Schamz.*

JOSHUA COHEN, *Witz.*

EMILY HOLMES COLEMAN, *The Shutter of Snow.*

ERIC CHEVILLARD, *The Author and Me.*

ROBERT COOVER, *A Night at the Movies.*

STANLEY CRAWFORD, *Log of the S.S. The Mrs Unguentine.*
Some Instructions to My Wife.

RENÉ CREVEL, *Putting My Foot in It.*

RALPH CUSACK, *Cadenza.*

NICHOLAS DELBANCO, *Sherbrookes.*
The Count of Concord.

NIGEL DENNIS, *Cards of Identity.*

PETER DIMOCK, *A Short Rhetoric for Leaving the Family.*

ARIEL DORFMAN, *Konfidenz.*

COLEMAN DOWELL, *Island People.*
Too Much Flesh and Jabez.

ARKADII DRAGOMOSHCHENKO, *Dust.*

RIKKI DUCORNET, *Phosphor in Dreamland.*
The Complete Butcher's Tales.

RIKKI DUCORNET (cont.), *The Jade Cabinet.*
The Fountains of Neptune.

WILLIAM EASTLAKE, *The Bamboo Bed.*
Castle Keep.
Lyric of the Circle Heart.

JEAN ECHENOZ, *Chopin's Move.*

STANLEY ELKIN, *A Bad Man.*
Criers and Kibitzers, Kibitzers and Criers.
The Dick Gibson Show.
The Franchiser.
The Living End.
Mrs. Ted Bliss.

FRANÇOIS EMMANUEL, *Invitation to a Voyage.*

PAUL EMOND, *The Dance of a Sham.*

SALVADOR ESPRIU, *Ariadne in the Grotesque Labyrinth.*

LESLIE A. FIEDLER, *Love and Death in the American Novel.*

JUAN FILLOY, *Op Oloop.*

ANDY FITCH, *Pop Poetics.*

GUSTAVE FLAUBERT, *Bouvard and Pécuchet.*

KASS FLEISHER, *Talking out of School.*

JON FOSSE, *Aliss at the Fire.*
Melancholy.

FORD MADOX FORD, *The March of Literature.*

MAX FRISCH, *I'm Not Stiller.*
Man in the Holocene.

CARLOS FUENTES, *Christopher Unborn.*
Distant Relations.
Terra Nostra.
Where the Air Is Clear.

TAKEHIKO FUKUNAGA, *Flowers of Grass.*

WILLIAM GADDIS, JR., *The Recognitions.*

JANICE GALLOWAY, *Foreign Parts.*
The Trick Is to Keep Breathing.

WILLIAM H. GASS, *Life Sentences.*
The Tunnel.
The World Within the Word.
Willie Masters' Lonesome Wife.

GÉRARD GAVARRY, *Hoppla! 1 2 3.*

ETIENNE GILSON, *The Arts of the Beautiful.*
Forms and Substances in the Arts.

C. S. GISCOMBE, *Giscome Road.*
Here.

DOUGLAS GLOVER, *Bad News of the Heart.*

WITOLD GOMBROWICZ, *A Kind of Testament.*

PAULO EMÍLIO SALES GOMES, *P's Three Women.*

GEORGI GOSPODINOV, *Natural Novel.*

JUAN GOYTISOLO, *Count Julian.*
Juan the Landless.
Makbara.
Marks of Identity.

HENRY GREEN, *Blindness.*
Concluding.
Doting.
Nothing.

JACK GREEN, *Fire the Bastards!*

JIŘÍ GRUŠA, *The Questionnaire.*

MELA HARTWIG, *Am I a Redundant Human Being?*

JOHN HAWKES, *The Passion Artist.*
Whistlejacket.

ELIZABETH HEIGHWAY, ED., *Contemporary Georgian Fiction.*

AIDAN HIGGINS, *Balcony of Europe.*
Blind Man's Bluff.
Bornholm Night-Ferry.
Langrishe, Go Down.
Scenes from a Receding Past.

KEIZO HINO, *Isle of Dreams.*

KAZUSHI HOSAKA, *Plainsong.*

ALDOUS HUXLEY, *Antic Hay.*
Point Counter Point.
Those Barren Leaves.
Time Must Have a Stop.

NAOYUKI II, *The Shadow of a Blue Cat.*

DRAGO JANČAR, *The Tree with No Name.*

MIKHEIL JAVAKHISHVILI, *Kvachi.*

GERT JONKE, *The Distant Sound.*
Homage to Czerny.
The System of Vienna.

JACQUES JOUET, *Mountain R.*
Savage.
Upstaged.
MIEKO KANAI, *The Word Book.*
YORAM KANIUK, *Life on Sandpaper.*
ZURAB KARUMIDZE, *Dagny.*
JOHN KELLY, *From Out of the City.*
HUGH KENNER, *Flaubert, Joyce and Beckett: The Stoic Comedians.*
Joyce's Voices.
DANILO KIŠ, *The Attic.*
The Lute and the Scars.
Psalm 44.
A Tomb for Boris Davidovich.
ANITA KONKKA, *A Fool's Paradise.*
GEORGE KONRÁD, *The City Builder.*
TADEUSZ KONWICKI, *A Minor Apocalypse.*
The Polish Complex.
ANNA KORDZAIA-SAMADASHVILI, *Me, Margarita.*
MENIS KOUMANDAREAS, *Koula.*
ELAINE KRAF, *The Princess of 72nd Street.*
JIM KRUSOE, *Iceland.*
AYSE KULIN, *Farewell: A Mansion in Occupied Istanbul.*
EMILIO LASCANO TEGUI, *On Elegance While Sleeping.*
ERIC LAURRENT, *Do Not Touch.*
VIOLETTE LEDUC, *La Bâtarde.*
EDOUARD LEVÉ, *Autoportrait.*
Newspaper.
Suicide.
Works.
MARIO LEVI, *Istanbul Was a Fairy Tale.*
DEBORAH LEVY, *Billy and Girl.*
JOSÉ LEZAMA LIMA, *Paradiso.*
ROSA LIKSOM, *Dark Paradise.*
OSMAN LINS, *Avalovara.*
The Queen of the Prisons of Greece.
FLORIAN LIPUŠ, *The Errors of Young Tjaž.*
GORDON LISH, *Peru.*
ALF MACLOCHLAINN, *Out of Focus.*
Past Habitual.
The Corpus in the Library.
RON LOEWINSOHN, *Magnetic Field(s).*
YURI LOTMAN, *Non-Memoirs.*
D. KEITH MANO, *Take Five.*
MINA LOY, *Stories and Essays of Mina Loy.*
MICHELINE AHARONIAN MARCOM, *A Brief History of Yes.*
The Mirror in the Well.
BEN MARCUS, *The Age of Wire and String.*
WALLACE MARKFIELD, *Teitlebaum's Window.*
DAVID MARKSON, *Reader's Block.*
Wittgenstein's Mistress.
CAROLE MASO, *AVA.*
HISAKI MATSUURA, *Triangle.*
LADISLAV MATEJKA & KRYSTYNA POMORSKA, EDS., *Readings in Russian Poetics: Formalist & Structuralist Views.*
HARRY MATHEWS, *Cigarettes.*
The Conversions.
The Human Country.
The Journalist.
My Life in CIA.
Singular Pleasures.
The Sinking of the Odradek.
Stadium.
Tlooth.
HISAKI MATSUURA, *Triangle.*
DONAL MCLAUGHLIN, *beheading the virgin mary, and other stories.*
JOSEPH MCELROY, *Night Soul and Other Stories.*
ABDELWAHAB MEDDEB, *Talismano.*
GERHARD MEIER, *Isle of the Dead.*
HERMAN MELVILLE, *The Confidence-Man.*
AMANDA MICHALOPOULOU, *I'd Like.*
STEVEN MILLHAUSER, *The Barnum Museum.*
In the Penny Arcade.
RALPH J. MILLS, JR., *Essays on Poetry.*
MOMUS, *The Book of Jokes.*
CHRISTINE MONTALBETTI, *The Origin of Man.*
Western.

NICHOLAS MOSLEY, *Accident.*
Assassins.
Catastrophe Practice.
A Garden of Trees.
Hopeful Monsters.
Imago Bird.
Inventing God.
Look at the Dark.
Metamorphosis.
Natalie Natalia.
Serpent.

WARREN MOTTE, *Fables of the Novel: French Fiction since 1990.*
Fiction Now: The French Novel in the 21st Century.
Mirror Gazing.
Oulipo: A Primer of Potential Literature.

GERALD MURNANE, *Barley Patch.*
Inland.

YVES NAVARRE, *Our Share of Time.*
Sweet Tooth.

DOROTHY NELSON, *In Night's City.*
Tar and Feathers.

ESHKOL NEVO, *Homesick.*

WILFRIDO D. NOLLEDO, *But for the Lovers.*

BORIS A. NOVAK, *The Master of Insomnia.*

FLANN O'BRIEN, *At Swim-Two-Birds.*
The Best of Myles.
The Dalkey Archive.
The Hard Life.
The Poor Mouth.
The Third Policeman.

CLAUDE OLLIER, *The Mise-en-Scène.*
Wert and the Life Without End.

PATRIK OUŘEDNÍK, *Europeana.*
The Opportune Moment, 1855.

BORIS PAHOR, *Necropolis.*

FERNANDO DEL PASO, *News from the Empire.*
Palinuro of Mexico.

ROBERT PINGET, *The Inquisitory.*
Mahu or The Material.
Trio.

MANUEL PUIG, *Betrayed by Rita Hayworth.*
The Buenos Aires Affair.
Heartbreak Tango.

RAYMOND QUENEAU, *The Last Days.*
Odile.
Pierrot Mon Ami.
Saint Glinglin.

ANN QUIN, *Berg.*
Passages.
Three.
Tripticks.

ISHMAEL REED, *The Free-Lance Pallbearers.*
The Last Days of Louisiana Red.
Ishmael Reed: The Plays.
Juice!
The Terrible Threes.
The Terrible Twos.
Yellow Back Radio Broke-Down.

JASIA REICHARDT, *15 Journeys Warsaw to London.*

JOÃO UBALDO RIBEIRO, *House of the Fortunate Buddhas.*

JEAN RICARDOU, *Place Names.*

RAINER MARIA RILKE, *The Notebooks of Malte Laurids Brigge.*

JULIÁN RÍOS, *The House of Ulysses.*
Larva: A Midsummer Night's Babel.
Poundemonium.

ALAIN ROBBE-GRILLET, *Project for a Revolution in New York.*
A Sentimental Novel.

AUGUSTO ROA BASTOS, *I the Supreme.*

DANIËL ROBBERECHTS, *Arriving in Avignon.*

JEAN ROLIN, *The Explosion of the Radiator Hose.*

OLIVIER ROLIN, *Hotel Crystal.*

ALIX CLEO ROUBAUD, *Alix's Journal.*

JACQUES ROUBAUD, *The Form of a City Changes Faster, Alas, Than the Human Heart.*
The Great Fire of London.
Hortense in Exile.
Hortense Is Abducted.
Mathematics: The Plurality of Worlds of Lewis.
Some Thing Black.

RAYMOND ROUSSEL, *Impressions of Africa.*

VEDRANA RUDAN, *Night.*

PABLO M. RUIZ, *Four Cold Chapters on the Possibility of Literature.*

GERMAN SADULAEV, *The Maya Pill.*

TOMAŽ ŠALAMUN, *Soy Realidad.*

LYDIE SALVAYRE, *The Company of Ghosts.*
The Lecture.
The Power of Flies.

LUIS RAFAEL SÁNCHEZ, *Macho Camacho's Beat.*

SEVERO SARDUY, *Cobra & Maitreya.*

NATHALIE SARRAUTE, *Do You Hear Them?*
Martereau.
The Planetarium.

STIG SÆTERBAKKEN, *Siamese.*
Self-Control.
Through the Night.

ARNO SCHMIDT, *Collected Novellas.*
Collected Stories.
Nobodaddy's Children.
Two Novels.

ASAF SCHURR, *Motti.*

GAIL SCOTT, *My Paris.*

DAMION SEARLS, *What We Were Doing and Where We Were Going.*

JUNE AKERS SEESE, *Is This What Other Women Feel Too?*

BERNARD SHARE, *Inish.*
Transit.

VIKTOR SHKLOVSKY, *Bowstring.*
Literature and Cinematography.
Theory of Prose.
Third Factory.
Zoo, or Letters Not about Love.

PIERRE SINIAC, *The Collaborators.*

KJERSTI A. SKOMSVOLD, *The Faster I Walk, the Smaller I Am.*

JOSEF ŠKVORECKÝ, *The Engineer of Human Souls.*

GILBERT SORRENTINO, *Aberration of Starlight.*
Blue Pastoral.
Crystal Vision.
Imaginative Qualities of Actual Things.
Mulligan Stew. Red the Fiend.
Steelwork.
Under the Shadow.

MARKO SOSIČ, *Ballerina, Ballerina.*

ANDRZEJ STASIUK, *Dukla.*
Fado.

GERTRUDE STEIN, *The Making of Americans.*
A Novel of Thank You.

LARS SVENDSEN, *A Philosophy of Evil.*

PIOTR SZEWC, *Annihilation.*

GONÇALO M. TAVARES, *A Man: Klaus Klump.*
Jerusalem.
Learning to Pray in the Age of Technique.

LUCIAN DAN TEODOROVICI, *Our Circus Presents . . .*

NIKANOR TERATOLOGEN, *Assisted Living.*

STEFAN THEMERSON, *Hobson's Island.*
The Mystery of the Sardine.
Tom Harris.

TAEKO TOMIOKA, *Building Waves.*

JOHN TOOMEY, *Sleepwalker.*

DUMITRU TSEPENEAG, *Hotel Europa.*
The Necessary Marriage.
Pigeon Post.
Vain Art of the Fugue.

ESTHER TUSQUETS, *Stranded.*

DUBRAVKA UGRESIC, *Lend Me Your Character.*
Thank You for Not Reading.

TOR ULVEN, *Replacement.*

MATI UNT, *Brecht at Night.*
Diary of a Blood Donor.
Things in the Night.

ÁLVARO URIBE & OLIVIA SEARS, EDS., *Best of Contemporary Mexican Fiction.*

ELOY URROZ, *Friction.*
The Obstacles.

LUISA VALENZUELA, *Dark Desires and the Others.*
He Who Searches.

PAUL VERHAEGHEN, *Omega Minor.*

BORIS VIAN, *Heartsnatcher.*

LLORENÇ VILLALONGA, *The Dolls' Room.*

TOOMAS VINT, *An Unending Landscape.*

ORNELA VORPSI, *The Country Where No One Ever Dies.*

AUSTRYN WAINHOUSE, *Hedyphagetica.*

CURTIS WHITE, *America's Magic Mountain.*
The Idea of Home.
Memories of My Father Watching TV.
Requiem.

DIANE WILLIAMS,
Excitability: Selected Stories.
Romancer Erector.

DOUGLAS WOOLF, *Wall to Wall.*
Ya! & John-Juan.

JAY WRIGHT, *Polynomials and Pollen.*
The Presentable Art of Reading Absence.

PHILIP WYLIE, *Generation of Vipers.*

MARGUERITE YOUNG, *Angel in the Forest.*
Miss MacIntosh, My Darling.

REYOUNG, *Unbabbling.*

VLADO ŽABOT, *The Succubus.*

ZORAN ŽIVKOVIĆ , *Hidden Camera.*

LOUIS ZUKOFSKY, *Collected Fiction.*

VITOMIL ZUPAN, *Minuet for Guitar.*

SCOTT ZWIREN, *God Head.*

AND MORE . . .